New Fiction

SUMMER FRUITS

Edited by

Rebecca Mee

First published in Great Britain in 2000 by
NEW FICTION
Remus House,
Coltsfoot Drive,
Peterborough, PE2 9JX
Telephone (01733) 898101
Fax (01733) 313524

SB ISBN 1 85929 022 1

FOREWORD

When 'New Fiction' ceased publishing there was much wailing and gnashing of teeth, the showcase for the short story had offered an opportunity for practitioners of the craft to demonstrate their talent.

Phoenix-like from the ashes, 'New Fiction' has risen with the sole purpose of bringing forth new and exciting short stories from new and exciting writers.

The art of the short story writer has been practised from ancient days, with many gifted writers producing small, but hauntingly memorable stories that linger in the imagination.

I believe this selection of stories will leave echoes in your mind for many days. Read on and enjoy the pleasure of that most perfect form of literature, the short story.

Parvus Est Bellus.

CONTENTS

Zapped	Trudi Danks	1
Too Busy Counting Magpies	Kevin Cowdall	7
Time Gentleman	Margaret Rose Harris	13
Belfast Echoes	Stan Howes	17
Yesterday	Valerie Warner	23
The Chair	Jennifer Polledri	26
The Drummer Boy	Jacki Larcombe	29
The Decision	Perry McDaid	36
Near Brockenhurst	Jo Young	39
The Star	H McLean	45
The Birthday	Susanne Shalders	48
A French Affair	F Jensen	51
The Ghost Chaser	Nicola Grant	55
Telynor	Gordon Vale	59
C U Later	Di Bagshawe	63
My Mother The Hero	Anthony Tamburro	68
Meeting Strangers	David Barnett	72
The Patchwork Quilt	Phyllis Spooner	76
Stranger On A Train	David Daniels	82
Scream To The Darkness	Paddy Jupp	85
Elsie Merry's Christmas	Ivy Squires	96
Illusion	Wilma Kenny	99
Apocalypse	Thomas Wignall	102
The Memory Shelf	Irene Constantine	117
Flashback	Rebecca Hardie	125
Together Forever	D Upson	128
The Girl I Married	Peter S A Cooper	131

ZAPPED
Trudi Danks

Saturday and the place was jammed.

I reached the DIY store and stood to one side, holding the door for a woman and young girl struggling out with tins of paint. As she passed, the woman hesitated, and said something to the girl.

I stared blankly and was about to walk on.

'Don't remember me James, do you?' The woman smiled. 'I've not changed that much, surely?'

Cathie Dobson. It was the voice I recognised and it must have been eight years since I'd last seen her.

We'd lived in the same street and she'd married one of my mates. After they moved we'd lost touch. Cathie was the one everybody fancied at school, a real stunner, and I could hardly believe how much she'd changed.

The face was drawn and haggard. Deep lines etched her forehead and her hair, a rich auburn as I remember it, was completely grey. She looked like an old woman.

I fumbled for my lighter and lit up a cigarette.

'Aye, I remember you Cathie. Away in a world on my own there. How's Rab? Still into his fishing at the weekends?'

The smile faded.

'Rab's dead. Heart attack, last October. My mum had a stroke and I moved back here to look after her.'

Christ. No wonder she looked the way she did. I looked at the girl standing beside her.

'This can't be the Laura . . . ?'

'Sure is. Fourteen now. Looks like her Dad doesn't she? Robert will be sixteen this year.' She pulled a face. 'Makes me feel old. What about you? Still doing your electrician?'

I nodded. Cathie continued:

'I've got this cooker. Second-hand like, and I'm needing it wired in.'

I took a card out of my top pocket.

'No problem. Just give me a phone.'

She phoned the following Wednesday and as I'd nothing else on, said I'd be up sometime after seven. My van was off the road and I decided rather than hang about waiting for a bus, I'd take the short cut over the fields. A ten minute walk at the most.

Daylight was fading as I climbed the steep path leading to the field. It's not a field in the true sense, a bit of spare ground is a better description and from there, on a clear night, you can see the whole of Glasgow. Tonight, only tower blocks, great monoliths silhouetted against the overcast sky were visible.

I found Cathie's house and Laura opened the door. She motioned for me to come in and as we made our way along the hall, raised voices came from the living room.

Cathie looked round as I entered. The bruise on her cheek and red-rimmed eyes said it all.

Beside her, a boy I took to be Robert, glanced at me without interest and sauntered over to the window. They were obviously having a row, a regular occurrence by the looks of it, and in an attempt to cover her embarrassment, Cathie lifted a newspaper, folded it and placed it on the coffee table. Avoiding my eyes she said:
'See you found us all right. Thanks for coming James. The cooker's through there.' Her hand shook as she pointed to the door on my left.
'Oh, by the way, this is young Robert.'
The boy did not turn round. Evidently he hadn't inherited his mother's good nature, or his father's. He continued to stare out of the window, then slamming his fist on the ledge, turned abruptly.

He was tall, well built like Rab, but looked nothing like him. Without a word he walked across. At the door he paused and looked straight at me. There was nothing friendly in the look, no recognition, even though he'd remember me from the times Rab and I took him fishing. His eyes were most unusual; a pale colour, cold, empty, and totally void of feeling. An odd sensation ran through me. I felt I was looking into the eyes of a snake. The outside door slammed and for several moments, no one said anything.

'Not very sociable our Robert.' Laura opened the door leading into the kitchen. Her hand gestured round. 'Bit of a state in here. The man just left the cooker sitting there.'

'Take it that's the space for it over by the unit?'

Laura nodded. I opened my tool bag and took out my socket set. Cathie came in. She stared at her feet. Her voice was quiet.

'I'm sorry about Robert. I don't know what's got into that boy. Sometimes I think he blames me . . . his dad . . . ' She struggled to control the tears. Laura cut in.

'Never mind him Mum.' She lifted the kettle. 'Anybody want tea?'

Cathie didn't appear to have heard. Lost in thought, she stared unseeingly out into the night, then she turned.

'Sorry James. Can I give you a hand with anything?'

I shook my head and flicked on my torch.

'Need to turn the power off for a couple of minutes.'

It was a straightforward enough job and all in, took about an hour. I'd just finished putting my tools away when Cathie came back through. She seemed pleased with the way I'd fitted the cooker and hood and asked if I'd like some tea. I stood up.

'Need to get back down the road. Linda's on shifts. Doesn't like coming back to an empty house. Thanks anyway.'

Cathie reached into the drawer and brought out her purse.

'You've made a good job of that. How much do I owe you?'

This was the part I hated. The place was spotless, but from the black and white TV set and worn carpet, I could tell she was struggling. No doubt the argument with the boy was over money.

'Look, I'm not wanting anything . . . for all the time it took.'

The colour rose in her cheeks and she put the purse back in the drawer.

'If you need anything else done, just give me a shout.'

'Thanks James, appreciate it. Robert's electric blanket's not working . . maybe you could have a quick look at it.'

I'd packed away my tools and electric blankets can be time consuming. More bother than they're worth usually.

'I've not got my neon tester, but get Laura or the boy to bring it round.'

She reached behind the door for her jacket.

'That's what I'll do. Now Laura, I'm just going over to your gran's for ten minutes. Keep that door locked till I get back. Wait and I'll get you down James.'

At the foot of the stairs she thanked me again. I watched the small figure hurry across the road then set off towards the field.

Cathie's back rooms overlooked the fields and Laura was standing at the window. She waved and I waved back. By now it was completely dark, scudding clouds revealing an occasional glimpse of a crescent moon. The lights of Glasgow stretched into the distance, twinkling and shimmering, reminding me of the time I'd sailed into Rio de Janeiro during my brief, but interesting, stint in the Merchant Navy. Cities, to me anyway, look more intriguing at night.

Halfway across the spare ground I lit a cigarette. A plane was coming in, hovering in the dark sky like a giant albatross. I watched it thunder along the runway, engines screaming.

The jangling strains of 'The Skater's Waltz' drifted up from an ice-cream van somewhere in the scheme and stubbing out my cigarette end, I lifted my tool bag. The wind had increased and it had become colder. I fastened my jacket and was about halfway across the field when I heard a scream, piercing, high-pitched, and although I couldn't be certain, I thought I heard someone call out my name. I spun round. Less than twenty yards away I could make out three figures walking purposefully towards me. One of them was carrying something in his right hand. To the right, two other figures were advancing steadily, abreast of the other three. In the dark it was difficult to tell, but they were probably around sixteen, seventeen at the most. Tall, heavy built, and menacing.

The voice in the distance was still calling out my name. It was Laura. She was trying to warn me. Like a pack of wolves, they closed in and formed a semi-circle around me. I half considered making a run for it but knew it was useless. Grasping the tool bag I turned and as I did, one of them ducked in at me back and the pickaxe handle hit me from behind, knocking me to the ground.

Everything happened so fast. One of them moved forward, grabbed my hair and pulled my face down. My teeth crunched as his boot hit my mouth. Blood dribbled down my chin. No one spoke. They methodically set about me. Teamwork. Boots connected with my ribs, head, chest. I heard my ribs crack, and thought I was going to throw up. My head felt as if it was about to explode. Everything went black and the tool bag was wrenched from my grip. Semi-conscious, I was vaguely aware of hands searching my pockets. Throughout, not a word was spoken. They knew what they were after.

It was probably the pain in my ribs which kept me from passing out altogether and I tried to focus on the guy rifling my trousers. And for the second time that night, the amber eyes held mine. Cold, deadly. Then I saw the glint of steel. Without changing his expression, he brought the knife down on to my chest, and although I felt the blow, oddly, I didn't feel any pain. At that point, I lost consciousness.

How long I stayed there I've no idea, but I remember hearing a police siren in the distance. Somebody dragged me to my feet, then promptly dropped me. Blood poured down my face and neck. My head and chest felt like they'd been hit by a bulldozer. Voices came and went, lights flickered and I was heaved, none too gently, into the back of a vehicle.

According to the doctor at the hospital, I was lucky. My stainless steel lighter stopped the blade from going through. Saved my life, he told Linda impartially.

Cathie and Laura came up to see me the following day and if Laura knew her brother was involved, she didn't say. Out of fear possibly, but she also knew her mother wouldn't be able to handle it.

Then the CID turned up and asked me all sorts of stupid questions. They made no attempt to conceal the fact that they thought I'd set the whole thing up to get a few bob in criminal injuries. I must have repeated my story half a dozen times, without mentioning Robert, but they were not interested and neither was I, and we left it at that.

While I'd been in there I'd done some serious thinking. Robert was definitely screwed up, a danger to himself as well as everybody else. I had the feeling Rab's death had a lot to do with it. A good hiding wouldn't solve anything, he'd be back on the street in no time. What he needed was a fright. Flat on his back for a couple of weeks. Time to think, get his priorities right, realise he didn't have to prove himself a hard man to his so-called friends. And I'd worked out just the way to do it.

I'd asked Laura to bring his electric blanket round once I got out of hospital. The one that needed fixing. I'd fix it alright.

TOO BUSY COUNTING MAGPIES
Kevin Cowdall

'Shit. Three.'

She watched the trio of magpies through the window of her car as they bobbed across the newly cut grass of the stretch of parkland bordering the road, amazed as always that such heavy, solid creatures could rise so easily, so languidly, into the air at the merest whim.

'Three. Shit. Three for a girl.'

Probably meant her first client would be some ditzy woman with a personal crisis and an overwhelming desire to unload, who would spend hours talking to her as if they were best friends and had known each other forever. Or the new temp would screw the photocopier up again and spill coffee over a couple of files. Again. Or her mother would ring to remind her that *she* hadn't phoned for ages (three weeks for God's sake!). Or -

'Shit!'

The brake pads gripped with an ear-grating screech and the car shuddered to a halt, missing the child by inches as she dashed from behind the parked van. For a moment there was one of those unreal, seemingly time-frozen tableaux; the little girl, five or six years old, standing in the middle of the road staring blankly at the driver through the web of tree branches reflected in the windscreen from overhead, she relaxing her white-knuckled grip of the steering wheel and letting out the pent-up breath in an exhale that blanked out everything for a second in a wave of relief.

'You stupid little bitch! What the . . . '

But the child had already stooped to pick up something she had dropped and moved off to the pavement across the way, seemingly oblivious, as only young children can be, to the potential tragedy and the demented banshee she had left trembling in her wake. Stopping after about fifty yards or so, she fumbled with the bag she had retrieved and started to scatter its contents on the grass around her. The three magpies hopped towards her unhesitatingly and began to peck at the white pellets of bread lying about them like so many cotton balls.

'For fuck's sake. Well I hope they choke. Stupid little bitch.'

She put the car in gear and drove on.

'Yes! Two. Two for joy.'

God knows, she could do with some of that.

'Two for joy. Now then, let me think. Two for joy. Two for joy. What would really, *really* make my day? What can I think of that would - fuuuuuck!

'For Christ's sake!'

'I don't believe this, I do not believe this!'

She wound the window down and leant out, but the little girl had moved across the road slightly and she found herself having to pull against the restraining seat belt in order to make eye contact and, given the awkward and uncomfortable position she was now struggling to hold, her next words lacked the impact and outrage she would have wanted.

'What the hell's the matter with you, you stupid brat. You trying to get yourself killed?'

The child merely shrugged and moved off.

She slumped back into her seat fuming with the girl and herself for the pathetic, flustered show. Angrily she glanced back across the road to the parkland and saw the girl, as the day before, feeding the birds. As if she sensed the glare, and, perhaps the seething thoughts behind it, the child looked up and then, after a moment, gave a brief wave of the hand.

'Of all the . . . '

She crunched the car back into gear and took off with a jerk that had the wheels screeching in protest.

'Two for joy, my arse.'

'Three. Again. Three for a girl - oh, yes and I know which particular bloody girl that's going to be. Well sod it, if it happens again I'm going to run the little bitch over and plead provocation. I'll . . . '

She slowed the car as the parked van, seemingly unmoved from its customary position, drew near and then, just for good measure, gave a series of blasts on the horn.

At the last moment, just as she moved past and was about to put her foot down, a tousled head of hair popped out from behind the van and, seeing the familiar car, gave a broad smile of recognition.

'You cheeky little . . . '

She slammed on the brakes and came to a halt a few yards further down the road. Winding down the window she leant out, remembering to undo the seat belt, and glared back at the young girl, still standing nonchalantly watching her, the faintest trace of the smile remaining despite the look on the woman's face.

'What the hell's the matter with you? Is it just me or do you try to wreck every passing motorist's nerves? Well, do I get an answer or are you deaf and dumb or what?'

The girl gave what could have been the merest nod of the head as the smile disappeared from her lips, or it might have been the beginning of some childish pout or sulk at the reprimand. Whatever, she cast a last brief look at the woman, then moved off around the back of the car towards the park and the waiting magpies.

'Well!'

She drove on in a silent rage.

'Deaf and dumb or what? How politically correct of me. What is it now? Hearing and speech impaired? Conversationally restricted? Communicationally challenged? I lose track with it all.'

The image of the child's face, the look of recognition and the smile, came back to her. Then the look of disappointment and upset, was it, at the harsh outburst? Deaf and dumb. Was she? *Had* she actually nodded? No, of course not, how could she hear what I was saying if she was deaf, you idiot? Lip read? *Could* children that young lip read? What am I doing?'

She shook her head to clear the thoughts and for a moment was able to concentrate on the day ahead. But the image of the little girl came back to her intermittently and she was unable to completely rid herself of it for the rest of the day.

'Late. And I bet there's only one frigging magpie this morning as well.'

She drew close and slowed as she came level with the familiar patch of parkland. The young girl was already there, feeding the birds - and there were five, no six of them.

'Six for gold. Yes. Good day ahead.'

Her thoughts were cut short as she found the child staring across at her, the expression on her face blank and unfathomable, steady and unblinking. After a moment's hesitation she raised a hand and gave a brief wave and was genuinely pleased when the girl, after a short hesitation of her own, returned it and smiled.

'Shit, what the hell. Six for gold. It was going to be a *goood* day.'

'Come on. Eight hours to go and then the weekend. Yes! Three whole days of lounging around the garden drinking, snacking, reading, music blaring to annoy the neighbours, and soaking up the sun. If the weather lasted. Bank holiday weekend - bound to rain. Two, let there be two.'

the car turned the corner and she slowed to scan the open spaces between the trees, disappointed at first, then brightening as she saw first one then two magpies hopping across the grass.

'Yes! Yes, yes, yes!'

Instinctively, one eye still on the birds, she slowed as she neared the parked van, then came to a halt as the young girl's head peered around the corner of the vehicle, a broad smile spreading across her face as she recognised the now familiar car and driver. She smiled back and waited for the child to cross the road, but the girl remained where she was. For several moments she simply stood there, then she made a brief gesture with one finger, motioning for her to bring the car forward a few feet. Curious, she eased the car forward a yard or so and pressed the button to wind the window down.

The smile spreading even further across her face, the girl brought her other hand out from behind her back to reveal a small cardboard plate with a piece of cake in the middle. The plate was decorated with whirls and blobs of bright colour, party plates were they called? And the cake matched the garishness; soft white icing with pink swirls over a sponge gooey with jam and cream.

It took a moment for her to understand and then she was genuinely touched.

'For me?'

The girl nodded.

'Your birthday?'

Again a nod, then one hand raised with all fingers extended and the other hand, clutching the bag of bread for the birds, with a single finger held alongside.

'You're six! Well done, happy birthday!' Then a silence as she struggled with her thoughts to find something else to say.

'What else can you say to a six-year-old child? Presents! Ask her what she got for her birthday, you idiot.'

But her embarrassment was avoided as the child, in the way of children, suddenly took off, racing across the road to the park. She turned briefly to give a wave, then moved off towards the birds.

She watched as the girl undid the bag and began to break up the slices of bread and scatter them.

'Quick, keep it at two.' She placed the plate on the passenger seat beside her and closed the window. As she put the car in gear she made a positive decision to go out and get the child a present at lunchtime, or at least send somebody out for something. Something small but meaningful that the girl could cherish, a book perhaps, or . . . or . . . she'd think of something. And if not, Melissa would know; had a whole brood of snot-nosed brats and was forever buying stuff to bribe them with.

'What a weekend!' She rolled her head to relieve the stiffness in the back of her neck caused by the sunburn and hoped the new white top she had bought showed off the tan to its best. She was toying with the idea of perhaps booking a few sessions at the local solarium for when it began to fade, as she turned the corner and automatically began to scan the parkland across the way. Her eye was suddenly caught by the cordon of orange and white cones sealing off half the road width. She slowed to pass around them, noticing with growing alarm the damage to the van, heavily dented and scraped along its side, when a police officer stepped out, busily winding up a length of striped plastic tape into a rough ball. She came to an abrupt halt and quickly wound down the window.

The policeman, a heavy set, experienced officer in his late forties, watched her approach as he tied up the last of the tape, noticing her curiosity, and moving nearer so that he was beside the car as the window came down.

'Yes miss, can I help you?'

'Has there been an accident? The question came heavily, her mind whirling with thoughts and images she did not want to hold.

'Do you come along here regularly?'

'Yes,' then, defensively, 'sometimes.'

He stood scrutinising her and she felt intimidated by his gaze despite herself and had to force herself to hold his gaze steadily. After a moment he relented.

'Little girl got hit by a car over the weekend.' He paused to indicate the van. 'Ran out from behind there. Driver swerved to avoid her, hit the van there and caught her side on.'

She had to force the words out and they came hesitantly. 'Is she okay?'

'A couple of broken bones, leg and arm, and a few cuts and bruises. Nothing serious. Rushed her straight to hospital and patched her up. Hopefully taught her a lesson.'

Her relief was evident and caught his curiosity.

'You say you come along her fairly often then?'

'Fairly regularly if I'm going into the office. I think I may have seen the girl sometimes feeding the birds in the park there. Bit ghoulish of me to stop, sorry. So long as she's okay, that's the main thing.'

'Oh, she'll be fine in a few weeks I expect. Deaf she is, no speech either, poor little mite. Driver was fairly shaken up from all accounts.' He paused as if turning the next sentence over, mulling it in his mind, then continued. 'Weird really, obviously the little girl's fault, just running out without looking, but the driver said he didn't see her until the last second. Said he was too busy counting magpies.'

'What?'

He mistook her reaction and repeated himself. 'Too busy counting magpies. Over there, look.' He pointed across the road and she turned to follow where he indicated - the thought in her mind even as she focused - and saw the birds between the trees.

'Two, thank God!'

'Reckons he counts them every time he passes by to see what sort of day it's going to be, if you can believe it. You know the old nursery rhyme - one for sorrow, two - '

'Two for joy. Yes, yes I remember it.'

A silence fell between the two.

'Well, I'd best be going, running late as it is.'

'Very well miss, drive carefully now.'

He stood back as she put the car in gear and eased away.

'Fuck!'

She glanced to the seat beside her at the elaborately wrapped present and thought that perhaps she could pop into the hospital with it.

'Too busy counting magpies, Jesus! And it could have been me, the times I just missed her! That's it, no more counting bloody magpies.'

She put her foot down and the car moved off along the road. Behind her the policeman tossed the used tape into a nearby litter bin and moved off towards the parked patrol car.

Across the road, on the stretch of parkland, beneath the shade of the trees, several more magpies swooped down, attracted by the pecking of the two already there.

TIME GENTLEMAN
Margaret Rose Harris

I was lying on the bed feeling bad when the knock came at the door. I struggled up and opened it and there he was - The Angel of Death. At first I didn't cotton on, even though his wings were all blowing in the wind. When I did, I can't say I was overjoyed. Anyway, he came into my dump (I have to call it that if I'm honest) and we stood and looked at each other for a bit.

'Sit down,' I said at last. I still had two chairs. The Angel of Death sat down. 'Have a drink,' I said.
'I wouldn't touch the stuff you've been drinking with a barge pole' he told me.
That kind of knocked me back, the nasty way he said it.
'What's wrong with cider then?' I asked.
'Cider and meths,' he said. 'Cider *and meths.*'
'OK' I told him, 'if that's the way you feel.'
'How do *you* feel?' he asked in a superior kind of voice.
'What do you mean, how do I feel?' I said. 'I feel - well, I feel *unprepared* if you want to know. I feel I've been taken advantage of.' I began to get worked up. 'It gives a guy a cold shiver' I said, 'to open the door and find somebody standing there telling you he's The Angel of Death. Listen,' I said 'are you sure you're not just a guy that's lost his way to a fancy dress party?'

The Angel of Death looked at me in a contemptuous way and blew a spiral of smoke. It floated up and spelled the word *ANGEL* in capitals.
'OK. OK,' I told him 'you've proved your point.'
'Come on then,' he said 'let's be off.'
'Now listen,' I said, 'it's not all that easy. I'm not in the mood. I'm OK as I am.'
'You' said The Angel of Death 'are about as un-OK a character as I've had to pick up.' He sniffed. 'Filthy' he said. 'Hideous smell - old beer, cider, meths bottles, hypo syringe, the lot. It's a shambles.'
'Alright, alright,' I said 'I know it's not a palace.'
'And look at you,' he went on, 'when did you wash last? Sleep between clean sheets, eat - ?'
'I had some fish and chips the other night,' I butted in. I felt incensed.

The Angel Of Death sat and looked at me as if I was dirt beneath his long flowing robe. I couldn't see if he had any feet, the damned thing was too long.

'Anyway,' I said, 'how did you plan to take me? Where's my chariot of fire?'

He looked bored. I didn't take to him at all.

'We don't keep chariots for the likes of you,' he said, 'they're for VIPs.'

That really got me mad.

'Listen,' I told him, 'I always understood if there *was* a heaven, it was equal rights for everybody. *Equal rights.* So how come I'm not allowed a chariot? Tell me that.'

'You will learn all in good time,' said the Angel. 'Come along, we should leave now.'

I could tell he was in earnest so I racked my brains. I didn't feel like leaving my slummy room. It wasn't much cop but I'd got used to it. One can get used to a lot.

Then I hit on it. It was something I'd been saving (like a kind of dream) for the time when this Salvation Army dame would come and share it with me. The one who'd fed me soup on the coldest nights. The one with the gentle smile. But the situation seemed desperate.

'Listen,' I said, 'I've got something we might share. It's special. There's not much but it's good.' And I climbed on a chair and got the small bottle of cherry brandy wrapped in dusty newspaper from the top of the cupboard. God knows the times I'd screamed inside for it, but I'd never got it down before. *It was my dream. It was my life-blood.*

'One for the road,' I said, 'here, take a sniff.'

The Angel took a sniff and his face gave out a kind of frosty smile.

'It'll warm us for the journey,' I told him, 'here, drink up.' I poured a small share for myself into a dirty, cracked tumbler and gave him the bottle.

'Thanks,' he said. First decent word since he'd come in. He took a sip and I could tell he enjoyed it.

It struck me as kind of funny, the two of us sitting there, the Angel with his long white wings waving away at his shoulders and his long white robe billowing all round him and me in my old jeans and vest that said *'WAG'* on the front. The *'NER'* part of it had gone somehow. I had no shoes on and my feet didn't look too clean. I guess we were a kind of contrast.

Suddenly I had a positive feeling I didn't want to go. I wanted to stay and dream about my salvation with the Salvation Army dame. What if I couldn't dream anymore where he reckoned on taking me.
'Look,' I said, (matey stuff), 'It's a cold night. What if I slip to the end of the road and pick up a big bottle of this stuff? We could get to know each other, let our hair down.'
The Angel of Death looked at me. 'Your hair is nearly at your waist already,' he said. 'And' he followed on, 'you have not the money to buy a bag of crisps, let alone cherry brandy.' He seemed to know everything about me. I didn't like it. I mean everybody has to have something secret nobody else knows about. That's why I'd hung on to my bottle on top of the cupboard so long.

A line of something came into my head. 'Unspotted from the world, in spite of doom mine own'. I seemed to remember old Cyrano de Bergerac said it when he was on the point of taking off. I felt proud for remembering but I didn't want it to be my taking off line as well. I had to get this gloom Angel character to stay on a while. And there wasn't much brandy left.

Then all of a sudden *she* came in. Right into my dirty, smelly old room, with her neat uniform and her gentle smile. He must have left the door open because she had no trouble there.
'You're just in time,' I said, 'my lovely, my love. I was frightened.' To my surprise she came right over to me and put both her arms around me as if she would protect me from the whole world and heaven and hell itself. I closed my eyes from the wonder of it. Then when I opened them again she had gone. Had I dreamed her? Had she really come in?

The Angel of Death suddenly looked at me quite kindly.
'It's no good you know,' he said. 'Your time's up.'
'It's not,' I cried wildly, 'look, what if I swore to you I'd cut out the old dope and the meths and all that jazz and go out and get a job? How would it be?'

'You know there's not a hope,' he said and he looked sad and wise. 'You do know, don't you?' He looked different. Either the swigs of cherry brandy had worked wonders on him or I hadn't taken him in properly when he first arrived.

'Drink up,' he told me, 'it's time.'

And so I took the last sip and we both stood up. The door of my room flew wide open before us and we stepped out into the darkness together.

* * * * * * *

'Is it blood?' said the girl and her face was pale.

'No,' said the burly man in the Salvation Army uniform, 'of all things, it's cherry brandy. He must have stolen it somewhere.' He looked down at the young man, one hand still clutching the top of the broken bottle. 'Reckon he was trying to climb up there and lost his balance. Funny thing you should have thought of looking in here tonight Sarah.'

'He looked so ill yesterday,' said the girl, 'and when he didn't come for some soup today, I was worried. It's awful that we were too late.'

'Don't blame yourself,' the man said, 'he'd been killing himself gradually for months. Nobody could have helped him.'

'But I wish,' she said 'oh I wish he hadn't been all alone at the end.'

BELFAST ECHOES
Stan Howes

'You're not!'

'I am!'

'You're not sorry! I know it in your voice when you're not sorry!'

'I think we should talk about this.'

Danny felt like a man who was slowly drowning and could do nothing to save himself.

'If we talked about it we could sort it out. Be reasonable.'

'Be reasonable! Be reasonable!' Lorna's pitch rose with each syllable. She could always extract maximum impact from the fewest of words. She should have been an actress. 'You think everything can be cured by talking.'

'I think we should try it.'

'All you ever want to do is talk.'

Danny knew that an appeal to rationality usually rebounded. Still, he had to make the effort.

'It's all we've got. Let's discuss it in a calm, sensible way.'

'Now you're mocking me.'

'I'm not mocking you. I'm just trying to resolve, put right, what you think has gone wrong.'

'So you admit something has gone wrong between us.'

'I don't admit to anything of the kind. I would just like to understand. that's not asking too much.'

'If only you'd say sorry.'

'But I did!'

Danny pondered his words and wondered if he really did sound insincere. If this was insincerity what would sincerity sound like? As usual with Lorna she explained his directness as a clever deceit. Perhaps if he were deceitful she would believe him. As he thought this over Lorna shrugged in disgust and walked off into the night. He was tempted to scurry after her to plead his case, but realised being apart for a while might clear the air.

They had been wandering back from the pub after a trip to the cinema. It was one of those rare occasions when they had found a babysitter. The evening had gone incredibly well until they bumped into an old flame of Danny's in the mad chatter of The Crown Bar. He hadn't seen the girl for years. It would have been grossly impolite to have ignored her. Like most rows he had with Lorna, the alleged cause usually turned out to be a pretext, an excuse to row about something else. In this he could not absolve himself. They seemed to row a lot now, for no obvious reasons.

His reflection over, he realised he had crossed the Lagan River and had strayed into the long-forgotten territory of his youth. Suddenly memory stirred. When was it? Mid-seventies perhaps. He had a picture in his head of his art student brother, Kevin, bearded and with the cynicism of his nineteen years, pontificating on life and art while they drank his home-brewed beer and listened to Neil Young or King Crimson on a decrepit stereo.

He recalled that beer with graphic horror. It was the sort of cloudy, murky ooze that left you with a day-long hangover and the bitter but futile resolve never to drink it again. Many a night he had ended up studying the lavatory bowl in his brother's flat in one of those emptily pensive states of mind. There were nights too, when he would wake to the sounds of the nearby bakery; the hum of machinery and the desolate shouts of men. Sleepless in the small hours, he would muse on the great issues of life and death.

In the dawn there were the conversations with Kevin, tousle-haired and hungover, but with the flame of creativity still sputtering through his drowse. He talked with post-party hoarseness about his next exhibition that would make his name, his reputation. They would have to acknowledge him someday. Were they all cretins? Couldn't they recognise talent?

And the walk home as the city made its first murmurs: the rattles, bangs, cacophonies. And the smells of diesel traffic mixing with wet leaves and the bracing breath of a new day washed of night shadows.

They had been good times though, thought Danny. A period of life when you could still dream about the future, have plans and lofty aspirations.

It was a time when girls meant more than marriage and kids. They seemed to promise something indefinable, something you couldn't quite put your finger on. He remembered the vivid ethnic-style dresses so beloved by hippies and the long braided hair. They were like Pre-Raphaelite beauties.

It was a period for indulging in half-baked ideas and philosophies and reading obscure poets. Rimbaud was one such; a poet who lived a commendably short and intense life as poets should. He could never make head or tail of his poetry though, but it was the sort of volume to be seen with. We were right posers thought Danny with a wry smile.

When not partying lethally on his brother's head-rending brew they used to go for cycle rides along the Lagan towpath on summer days: Danny, Kevin, his girlfriend and sometimes a hippie friend called Mike when he was lucid enough to pedal. They would take-off in the direction of Shaw's Bridge where the trees strewed blotches of shadow on the white, winding path and sometimes a flotilla of swans would cruise by in regal silence or red-billed moor hens dithered and dived. There were old locks to explore where water burbled and gurgled in weed-dark, fish-darting pools overhung with ferns, the lock gates splintering and soft with rot.

They would find some secluded, shady spot to contemplate life which seemed then a forever experience. He remembered one day or was it many days rolled into one? It didn't matter. There was his brother asleep in the grass, a fly buzzing around his nose, his brother's girlfriend with her long, wavy hair, Mike, a little apart, smoking contentedly, and before them the river sliding slowly, effortlessly around a tree-dangling bend. It was not necessary to know what lurked around that bend. 'Be happy in the moment,' his brother would say.

'Do you have the time mate?' asked a stranger abruptly.

'Nineteen seventy . . . sorry. Eleven o'clock.'

'Are you OK mate? Not thinking of doing anything silly?' The stranger nodded to the river.

'Wouldn't think of it. Knowing my luck I'd float!'

'Never as bad as that,' said the stranger. 'There's always tomorrow.'

Danny was not thinking of tomorrow for he had suddenly got the urge to seek out his brother's old lodgings. They couldn't be more than a few minutes walk from where he stood. Excitement jostled with curiosity. It would be wonderful to see the old place again. He roamed the damp, tree-lined streets looking for anything familiar, anything that would square with memory. It was only fifteen years before but how different everything looked. Then he saw a street he recognised .He knew if he followed it and turned left at the bottom of the road by the library he would reach his goal.

He trembled with anticipation as he entered the old, not so familiar street and began counting off the terrace house numbers: thirty-seven, thirty-eight, thirty-nine . . . where was forty? He couldn't have miscounted. A new, many windowed building towered before him. It was dark and anonymous and dwarfed the neighbouring properties. He went up the steps and peered at the polished name plate. It belonged to some international oil company. His brother's flat was no more. It had been re-developed!

A chill regret took hold. It was as if that drawer of tidily arranged memories had been brutally flung out. He spun round to look at the whole street and clutch at a fast-receding past. What a blissful, far-off land it had become. In the lamplight everything was quite commonplace and unremarkable. Hardly the starting point for youthful hopes. And yet it had been just that.

He thought then of his brother Kevin. The drinking and partying of his student days had given way to quiet respectability. While the recognition he craved had largely eluded him he managed to make an adequate living from his art in some sleepy town in England. As for Mike it wasn't drugs that were his undoing or alcohol. (He once saw him breakfast on a banana and half a bottle of vodka.) No. It had been one of those senseless bomb explosions of the seventies, that had caught him on his way to his favourite record shop to buy the latest album. When not indulging Mike had been a brilliant mechanic. Someone who, if turned loose in a scrapyard, could have conjured up a limousine. They had mourned Mike like the end of an era and for them it was. With his death life seemed to lose some of its shimmer.

Danny re-traced his steps. An inner voice was saying: never go back. I told you so. It's always a mistake to go back. Things can never be what they were.

He could see the river again, dark but for the street lights twisting on its black surface and disappearing around another bend, a bend he did not want to think about. Where had it all gone: the dreams and the ambitions? Was life the ultimate con? Looking on the glinting swirls slowly quietened him. Maybe there was a peace, a purpose to be had from that unending stream that had meandered through his life as it had meandered through the lives of others for hundreds, even thousands of years. People who were nameless and unknown had come and gone, their lives unmarked. They had vanished from the face of the earth. And yet it didn't matter. They had known the joy and the sadness. The joy and the sadness he repeated. It was like the start of a poem. A poem without an ending.

The city appeared to recede and diminish leaving him alone with this silent, uncomplaining and strangely knowing companion. A companion that seemed to guess his thoughts and emotions without surprise or censure. He didn't have to explain himself, justify or make excuses. For once he was understood.

He woke on a park bench feeling stiff, cold and slightly hungover. It was about five in the morning; a grey light wafted through the trees. It had been bird song curiously mixed with the strains of King Crimson that had stirred him. He listened intently trying to catch the words of the song until only the twitter of birds remained. For a few moments he was in that uneasy, exciting state of wondering where, why, when and who he was. Then the previous night began flooding back and panic set in. God, what would Lorna be thinking? She would be worried sick!

When he got home Lorna was dozing on the couch. She seemed to have forgotten their quarrelsome words or chose not to mention them for she offered to make some breakfast.

'Where did you get to?' she asked while filling the kettle.

'Just walking.'

'You must have gone somewhere.'

'Nowhere in particular. Just wandering the streets and looking at houses.'

'For six hours? I thought you were never coming back.'

He was surprised by a spasm of emotion in her voice which made him look up from the kitchen table. She suddenly looked weak and older than of late. Her long delicate neck was bowed as if in some secret sorrow. He went over to her and slipped his arms around her waist.

'I thought you were never coming back,' she said again with tears in her eyes.

'I'm back . . . I'm back . . .' he murmured. 'You know I wouldn't leave you.'

'There isn't anyone else?'

'No. No one else.'

'Honest?'

'There was never anyone else.'

Running his hand through her hair he noticed its length. It was short; not a bit like the Pre-Raphaelite locks she once had, when she was his brother's girlfriend.

YESTERDAY

(Dedicated to Linda 1993)
Valerie Warner

She woke suddenly, from a fitful sleep and stared for a second or two at the unfamiliar cream-coloured door in front of her. Where was she - was she still dreaming?

Suddenly, her whole being screamed with awareness, as she ran her hands over her bruised and aching body, while she slowly realised that this was no dream after all and the tears flowed as she remembered yesterday. Was it really only yesterday that they had met for the first and last time? It seemed more like a lifetime ago - and now he was gone!

For most of her adult years she had dreamed of how he might look. She imagined his hair to be dark and curly. His eyes would be blue and his body would be long and slim. He would be everything that any girl might dream of. She would imagine how proud she would feel to walk down the street holding his hand; the envy of everyone around them. But now her dream was over for he was gone. All she had left were her thoughts and the mementoes in the envelope on her beside table. She reached for these, and as she gazed at them through her tear-stained eyes, the thoughts of what might have been went round and round and round inside her aching head.

She wiped her eyes on the corner of the sheet, but still the tears continued to slip uncontrollably from her swollen eyes, soaking into her pillow.

Her mind was silently screaming. Why? Why me? Why us? Was it only yesterday that I was still happy? But she was also very aware that now he was gone - forever!

She recalled once more, the very first time she had seen him. It was on the small screen and she remembered thinking 'there he is, *this* is the one I have waited for all my life', and feelings of love had overwhelmed her instantly. Each time he waved his hand about it seemed as though he was waving only to her, as though he knew that she would be watching his every move. And she was!

It has been surprisingly easy to 'talk' to him after that, and soon it became a daily occurrence. Over the next few months she had 'told' him all her secrets; all her hopes, her dreams, her fears - everything; while she continued to daydream of the time they would actually meet. But now he had gone - forever! How could she continue through life knowing that after their first brief meeting she would never see him or hold his dear hand ever again? The memories crowded again into her mind whilst the tears still flowed, unchecked from her eyes.

Yesterday! That had been the day they were destined to meet, after all the waiting, hoping and dreaming. Yesterday! The date was imprinted forever on her mind!

She had chosen their first meeting place herself; carefully, because this was going to be something very special. It was an old rambling building with an imposing entrance and as she had emerged from the taxi, she had stared around her, wondering how long he would keep her waiting. All at once, her feelings had overwhelmed her and she felt sick with apprehension and fear of the unknown, as she realised with certainty that her life would never be the same again after this first meeting! A uniformed figure had emerged from the building, ushering her quickly through the door and eventually into this room in which they were finally to meet.

He hadn't kept her waiting long and in reality, he was just as she had imagined. He was slim and dark-haired and his limbs were long and beautiful. They had lain naked on this bed, on which she now lay alone with only her memories and mementoes of yesterday.

She had thought that he was perfect in every way, for she had examined every precious inch of him; his face, his hands, his feet, his toes, his nails - everything. She had spoken to him softly, calling him by the pet name she had become accustomed to over the past few months, but he couldn't answer and now she would never hear his voice telling her he loved her, never see him smile, or hold his hand again. Not now, not ever! The light from her life had disappeared - yesterday.

She opened the envelope containing the photographs of her tiny son and gazed again at his beautiful face through her tear-filled eyes. The nurses had been so kind, and had even given her cards on which his tiny perfect foot had been imprinted.

Grief overwhelmed her once more and she turned, sobbing into her pillow, knowing that her life could never be the same again and that no-one could ever take the place of her precious son, who was stillborn - yesterday.

THE CHAIR
Jennifer Polledri

'Escaped prisoner on the loose.'

Arthur smiled to himself visualising the headlines in the daily tabloids. He gently stroked his white beard, reminding himself once again that he was the other side of 88 and although he wasn't actually locked up, he did feel like a prisoner at times.

Tom and Mabel said they could no longer look after him. 'Too much trouble,' commented Tom gruffly. What they really meant was that they wanted to put him into a home. Forget about him and all that. Arthur wasn't having it so he decided to rebel. He wanted his freedom and the right to come and go as he pleased.

After all, it didn't seem so long ago that he was a well-respected partner in a firm of solicitors. People used to treat him with respect. Acknowledge his expertise. Mabel and Tom made him feel his age, an old man, inadequate, who couldn't even walk about unaided.

Arthur reflected back for a moment. He remembered Peggy, his secretary, whom he later realised he didn't really appreciate at the time. On looking back, her cockney sense of humour was like a breath of fresh air in the office. She often used to say to Arthur, 'It must be being so miserable that keeps you going!' Well, thought Arthur, I was a miserable old so-and-so, grumpy, moody, pessimistic and I always did have trouble smiling. Then Arthur suddenly felt saddened as he thought of his dear wife, Sarah, who had passed away some years previously. She used to say jokingly that if he ever came back again, she hoped it would be as a nightingale, 'sweet'. 'I wouldn't be that lucky,' sighed Arthur.

'Anyhow, to the future,' he thought, brushing away the past. Today was the beginning of his 'new' life. His 'chair' was due to arrive shortly. He had looked forward to its arrival with some trepidation, then optimism and finally nervousness. Arthur was going out to face the world, a new man.

A knock on the door broke into his silent thoughts.

'I've arrived Mr King. Are you ready?' echoed a quiet voice from the other side.

'Come in,' said Arthur politely. He was reforming, slowly but surely.

The door opened and in came his new chair followed by a pretty blond woman.

'Hell-o,' she smiled, 'my name is Jacky and I've brought your wheelchair. Let me help you in and then off we'll go. It's a beautiful day!'

'Thank you,' replied Arthur, 'I've been looking forward to this *all* week.'

'Are you comfortable?' asked Jacky in soft tones.

'Fine,' said Arthur, 'absolutely fine,' nodding his head and placing his feet neatly on the metal frame underneath. Their walk took them along a street of newly built houses. Matchboxes, thought Arthur to himself, no character, no style. Then past a garage, across a busy road and down a winding path leading to a park.

Arthur loved the smell of the countryside and began to notice everything in more detail, treasuring its beauty. He was amazed he had never noticed such things before. Jacky was always pointing out new places for him to absorb.

There were the medley of ponds and streams that seemed to illuminate the landscape before him. Fields of golden daffodils and bell-shaped crimson tulips. His favourite white magnolia tree with its pure-white petals like children's hands in prayer. Trees were always one of Arthur's passions. He was intrigued with their gnarled barks covered with crusty patches and bushy growths, emulating branches that twisted into strange, disquieting shapes.

Sometimes, on an overcast day, Jacky used to take the wheelchair onto the bridge overlooking the railway. Arthur saw the railway as an intruder; massive and arrogant, disturbing the peace of the countryside like a magnificent, mechanical device that stretched out across the rolling downs. His precious trees that were once dignified and stately had become less to make way for the railway. He closed his eyes and listened. For a moment he was in time past. The steam train glowing with pride, brasswork gleaming, passed under the bridge as scruffy little boys sat on the grassy banks scribbling down its precious number.

People began to interest Arthur. Jacky took him into the towns where he discovered noise and crowds, impoverished ways that grated the senses. At first the people ignored him, he was not on their level, perhaps he didn't have a brain. Then he realised they were embarrassed because he was in a wheelchair. Arthur turned the tables. He would be in charge. So he started smiling at old ladies in bus queues, admired babies in prams, chatted to passers-by and in return he received warmth and acknowledgement. Arthur felt good, really good, for the first time in his life and even Mabel and Tom were nice to him.

He ordered a magnificent bouquet of red roses for Jacky for her kindness and understanding. She had taken him into a new world, a different world, and was even making plans to create a 'magical' garden for him.
'Just wait till the roses are in bloom next year,' said Jacky excitedly, 'then we can enter them in the flower show in July.'

But Arthur had a secret, a dark secret.
He wouldn't be here next July. The specialist had told him he had only six months to live, maybe less.

In the past few wonderful months, Arthur had learnt the most important lesson of his life. But it had almost come too late.
He was dying, yet in dying, he was learning to live.
It was a wonderful feeling.

THE DRUMMER BOY
Jacki Larcombe

His body was stretched out loosely across the soft fabric of the old sofa. Inert, head flung back, the only movement he made was to twirl the stuffing where it poked out of one of the numerous holes in the cloth with his fingers. Long legged and lean, he was clothed in black leather, thick silver chains and boots that made his feet look like Frankenstein's monster. His face in silhouette was thin and weary, as if where he was, was nothing to him except somewhere to rest. The room was cold and sparsely furnished. Other than the old sofa, there was a torn deck chair marked with salt, cast up from a raging sea long ago, somehow finding its way to this obscure city suburb and a scarred pine coffee table littered with empty beer cans and full ashtrays. A full moon cast silent icy fingers through the one remaining curtain, picking out the ravage of time; holes in bare floorboards, mouse droppings, piles of dust thick with dead spiders. Even when someone suddenly pounded on the street door below, nothing moved or stirred, other than the twitching nervous fingers.

In the street below a slim woman of unknown age banged on the door again. When there was no reply, she glared at her watch in the light cast by the full moon and saw that it was only 9 o'clock. She stepped back into the road so that she could look up at the window above her and as she did so she slipped in an icy puddle. Cursing, she brushed the wet sludge from her only good coat. Where was he she fumed, looking helplessly at the dark window where a ragged piece of red and white gingham hung bedraggled against the dark brick. She called him again, her voice harsh in the silent street, the echo of her voice reedy in the night shadows. Finally she gave up and moved reluctantly away from the house, occasionally turning her head back over her shoulder in the hope of seeing the light come on. When she reached the corner, she shrugged and turned away, heading for the taxi rank and home.

By the time Adrian stirred, it was long past midnight. He was cold and stiff and somehow aware of hunger yet unable to spend any energy in finding something to eat. Grunting he pushed himself up from the sofa and shuffled to the window, yanking the curtain down in disgust. It fell in a dusty heap onto the filthy floor where he pushed at it half-heartedly with his black boot. Had Emily come by as promised? He couldn't remember. Sighing he pushed his long fingers through his dark hair before peering into the dark street below. There was nothing there, only the sad spill of the street lights on wet pavements and far off the swish of cars on oily wet roads. Adrian sighed again and contemplated the dirty cold room. Had he come to this? He was only twenty-three, his whole life before him and yet all he had to show for it was this dirty squat in a back street London hole. Was it only a few short months since he had got a place at the Music College? He had left home so proudly, dragging his drum kit with him, setting up house with three other musicians; he had been so full of hope and promise back then. Pulling at his hair he moved back to the sagging sofa, collapsing in a heap. Before the first term was over his tutors had told him that he would never make a drummer. He was too undisciplined, too wild, too up front with his instrument. They made him take a back seat, pull in his elbows and play wrong-handed, at least for him. His dreams of playing wild passionate music slowly died and fizzled out. They didn't like how he looked, his punk rock clothes too stark amongst the jeans and T-shirts of the other students. But it had been the end of term 'show' that finished him off. Sitting there in the dark Adrian remembered the joy of putting a piece of music together, ignoring the dark looks thrown at him by his tutors and the hostile practice sessions. None of that had mattered once they had begun to play the music they'd written themselves, the lead guitar and the drums taking over with a wild passion that had the audience cheering. He remembered being flushed and proud again, ready to do anything, go anywhere. Instead they had expelled him. They had not listened to his arguments that if the audience liked his work, he was worth keeping on. They had turned deaf ears to his talent; if he was not prepared to play 'properly' they were not interested. Losing his temper, he had stormed from the Head's office, taken his drums home before packing a bag and leaving everything behind him. No one except Emily knew where he was. He thought of Emily, her long black hair, her soulful eyes and her small slim body. He didn't know why he had rung her and told her where he would be later; he didn't know what had possessed him to pour out his heart to her, all of it, his pain and anguish and his failure. But he knew now, in the dark and squalor of the room, that he couldn't face her anymore. He wasn't even sure if he could ever leave this room, again, let alone pick up a drumstick or bang a cymbal.

Emily sat in a back street coffee shop, a grey cup of tea in a thick china mug clasped in her hand. Her dark hair fell in her face and if anyone had looked at her closely, they would have seen she was crying. Adrian always made her cry. She'd known him for a year, loved him for six months. He was a difficult person to love. He was arrogant, yet sensitive. He suffered from paranoia and carried a huge chip on his shoulder about his parents' divorce. He demanded attention all the time, and when he drank he had the temper of a mad man. Emily had seen him totally trash a room in a matter of minutes. And yet behind that façade was a gentle, clever, talented lad who could turn any beat into an experience of the soul. They called him Animal, so wild was his drumming, but because it came from his heart it was always brilliant. She couldn't believe that the college had treated him so badly, and worse, he had lost his audition with *Saffron City* who at the behest of the club owner where they practised, only took students from the college. Emily sighed, it was all so unfair. What did it matter if Adrian used his whole body to play, or put his drum kit together back to front to the standard player? Who cared if he didn't play cross-armed or stiff shouldered? Finishing her tepid tea, Emily pushed her hair behind her ears and got up to go. She wouldn't give up on Adrian, not even if he gave up on himself. Somehow, somewhere, she'd make sure someone heard him play those drums, someone who counted for something, someone with clout. Banging the door behind her she stepped out into the night, heading back to Adrian's squat. She'd climb the drainpipe if necessary.

In the cold dark room at the squat, Adrian was still and silent, head flung back again, eyes closed.

Emily didn't see Adrian that night. There was no drainpipe and no way of getting into the squat.

The lead guitarist of *Saffron City* ticked off the last name on the audition list. None of the drummers had come anything close to what he wanted for the band. After a mad tour of the States, Alan their drummer had quit. He liked the money, but he didn't like the long nights, the different cities and the time spent away from Beth and the kids. Now

with a tour of Britain lined up, *Saffron City* had no drummer and the first gig at Wembley was only three weeks away. Rick banged his pen down in disgust. He never understood why he was obliged to audition college students - some were good sure, but too often they were too disciplined, too up tight. *Saffron City's* genre was wild rock, heady stuff that needed a drummer with soul and passion. He caught Den's eye and the base guitarist sauntered over from the coffee machine to join him and Jess. Rick looked at Den and Jess and sighed as he spoke,
'Let's hope tomorrow's lot have something to offer, otherwise we're going to have to cancel the tour.'

When Emily walked into college next morning, she saw Rick Honey the lead guitarist and singer from *Saffron City*. She and Adrian loved *Saffron City* and she couldn't believe he was here, although she knew there was a tour lined up for all the major British cities. He looked angry, his tousled fair hair sticking up on end where he had obviously continually pushed his fingers through it. His face was flushed and as he caught Emily's eye he frowned. Emily stiffened and pushed herself against the locker bay as he stormed past. A group of students were in a huddle, whispering together, their voices momentarily blotted out as Rick slammed the door behind him. As the group moved away, she saw Mr Taylor the music teacher, rip something from the notice board before flinging it in the bin. Emily retrieved it, smoothing out its colourful text. It was the audition ad for *Saffron City* advertising for a new drummer and by the look on Rick Honey's face they'd had no success. Adrian might still have a chance she thought, looking briefly towards the door still swinging from Rick's exit and ignoring the class bell ran from the building and out into the street, but there was no sign of Rick Honey anywhere. She had to get Adrian now and quickly.

Although daylight fell wanly through the squat window Adrian did not stir.

Emily, clutching a McDonald's take-away, stood weeping outside Adrian's window. Her hair and coat were soaked with rain and her voice harsh from calling his name over and over. Stiff with fear she had banged on the door for over half an hour, in the end trying to kick it in out of frustration and fear. The neighbourhood was still and deserted and when she looked right and left there was no life except for a black cat, which sat in a dignified pose on a crumbling wall. Finally, distraught Emily turned and ran back the way she had come dropping the brown McDonald's bag on the pavement. Clutching the torn and wrinkled *Saffron City* poster she knew what she had to do.

Rick, Den and Jess could hear shouting coming from the street even over the noise of the audition, a shrill voice rising and falling in what sounded like despair. Ignoring the mediocre drumming of the lad in front of him, Rick got up and walked towards the door that led to the alley. He was confronted with the club's bouncer clutching a screaming and kicking young woman, black hair falling in wild curls around her face.

'What is going on?' he roared and they both fell suddenly still. The bouncer dropped the girl who landed on her knees at Rick's feet. Pushing her hair from her face, she stood up, her chest heaving, tears spilling dirty tracks down her face. Now she was still, Rick could see that she was very young and beautiful.

'What is going on?' he repeated more quietly.

The bouncer, big and beefy, pushed in front of Emily, puffing with exertion.

'She says she's got to see you, about the drummer. I told her the auditions were closed and she tried to get by. No one gets by me,' he said, wheezing and clutching at his chest and glaring at the girl in front of him. Emily returned his glare almost spitting with rage.

'You didn't even give me a chance.' And then, turning to Rick she said, 'I know of a brilliant drummer, but we need to hurry.'

Rick hesitated, taking in the girl's panic, but beyond her panic he sensed excitement, an element of risk. Before he could change his mind he pulled her into the auditorium, trying to decipher what she was saying; something about some guy called Adrian, an animal drummer who had locked himself in a squat and wouldn't come out.

'Whoa' he finally said, pushing her down into a chair. 'Slowly, tell me slowly and we'll see what we can do.'

As Adrian stirred he realised that the pills had not worked. He could tell it was daylight, even through his closed eyes. He felt hot and ill, but still alive. He had been dreaming that he was playing his drums in front of a huge audience, sticks flying, dripping with sweat. Rick Honey from *Saffron City* had been there, cheering him on, shaking him with delight when he had finished playing. As he remembered that, he realised he *was* being shaken, his head lolling against the arm of the sofa, eyes glued shut with past hot tears and too much sleep. He could hear Emily's voice: 'Thank God he's alive' and a deeper male voice replying something he couldn't make out. Adrian forced his eyes open, let the pain of light filter through his pupils and into his brain. Light from the window threw Emily and her companion into silhouette, as if he had brought some demons back with him from the tortured land that he had inhabited for the last few days. Emily knelt down beside him and Adrian turned to look into her face, trying to hear what she was saying, but still aware of the tall silent visitor in front of him.

'You won't believe this Adrian, but Rick Honey is here. *Saffron City* still need a drummer,' she hissed in his ear.

Knowing that his image of the *Saffron City* lead guitarist was no dream, something in Adrian stirred. Long forgotten dreams of drumming to *Saffron City* in his stuffy bedroom, feeling the beat in his drums, the sweat in the line of his body as he played, pride in his own talent and with those memories came a lightness of spirit. He looked up at Rick and saw the anguish mirrored in the guitarist's eyes. Before he could move or stand up, before he could attempt to explain away the diminished room and the state he was in, Rick leant forward and took his hand.

'Right mate, I had to kick the door in to get to you, so you'd better be good. You've got two hours to bath and get something to eat, and then you drum. Emily will show you where to go. I'll see you then,' and without waiting for a reply, smoothly walked out of the squat as if it were a normal place for him to be. Adrian mutely looked at Emily and smiled.

The members of *Saffron City* watched Adrian play with something like awe on their faces. This was no ordinary drummer, no beat merchant who merely followed the other players. Adrian had talent, a gift that flowed through the wild gyrations of his body - it was part of him, just as his eyes or arms were. He played loosely, arms flying, elbows turned at impossible angles, head thrown back then forward with the joy of playing. They felt the beat of his drums up through their legs and arms, felt the thrill in their heads. There was no doubt that the lad had got the job, but they let him play on.

In the front row, Emily hugged herself, arms wrapped tightly across her chest. Above her on the stage, *Saffron City* were getting ready to play. The crowd was thick, nervous, worried that the great group would never be the same without Alan. They waited, tense and expectant.

Adrian sat behind his drums looking out at the vast crowd of Wembley. He felt the tension in the air, the nausea of adrenaline as it surged through his veins. He could feel the pulse of his heartbeat in his neck, his fingers itching to begin. For three weeks *Saffron City* (he still couldn't believe he was a part of *Saffron City* - it made him shiver with joy every time he thought about it) had spent every waking minute going over and over the same scores and songs until they were exhausted. Adrian had moved from the squat to Rick's house in St John's Wood, eating well and cleaning up his act. No drink, no pills. Nightmares of college and failure were far behind him, and if nothing else good ever happened to him again, he had those weeks and this night and all the days and hours of the tour ahead. He was here now watching the lights fall across Rick, glinting off his guitar and catching in Den and Jess's hair. He could feel the heat on his own face, the joy and terror of being a part of something big, something good. The voice of the compere boomed around the hall, echoing against the side of the stage as he announced *Saffron City*, Rick on the lead guitar, Jess on rhythm, Den on bass and Adrian the Animal on drums. Adrian felt the drum roll spin through his hands and cascade down across the skin of the drums. Then at a slight nod from Rick and on the count of four Adrian lifted his arms and played and inside his heart sang, while the crowd cheered and screamed.

THE DECISION
Perry McDaid

Paul drew the toe of his welly from the icky muck on the shore.

'Euck!' he exclaimed, wiping clean his favourite footwear on the nearby grass.

'What is it?' his sister asked.

His junior by some three years, Dinah had always looked to him for advice and leadership in a confusing world. Twelve himself, he had just started college and had already completed some projects on pollution - so he had a fair idea what the foul-smelling mire actually was.

'Pollution!' he answered, relishing the treat of dazzling her with science.

An attendant of a more progressive primary school than he had experienced at her age, she too had dabbled in such topics.

'Oh yeah,' she said through her bubblegum, 'we did that last week!'

Disappointed, Paul sighed - it was starting already. His days of being the wiser brother were numbered. Soon she would change into a horrible creature, intent on disagreeing with every word. He'd seen it happen to friends.

He decided to put his foot down, stamp out this terrible affliction before it took hold - perhaps it could be ridiculed into remission?

'What sort of pollution do *you* suppose it is?' he drawled sarcastically.

Dinah looked along the shore, then out to sea.

'Smelly stuff!' she said decidedly.

Paul was at a loss. How could you deliver a cutting response to such an innocent reply? He was ashamed of himself, and tried not to show it as her bright eyes regarded him expectantly.

'*Hoy!*' A tall figure ran towards them waving its arms. 'Get away from there!'

Paul nervously looked about for a stick, something with which to defend themselves. He could run, but Dinah was less fleet-footed and the ground was unsure.

The man stopped some way away.

'That stuff is poisonous!' the stranger said more calmly. 'Move away!'

Less alarmed now that the man had stopped running in their direction, Paul nodded to Dinah. Together they edged away from the black greasy mud which cluttered the shore.

Dinah shuddered as her foot dislodged a gull from its macabre resting place, but determinedly followed her brother as he retreated from the water's edge. The man followed at a non-threatening distance.

'It can soak through your skin!' the stranger imparted when they were clear. 'Give you *cancer*!' he added for effect.

'Cancer?' Dinah's eyes watered.

'You're frightening her!' Paul admonished. He was angry.

'It's frightening!' The man eyed the young girl disapprovingly. 'Don't mix with what you don't understand, youngster.' He regarded Paul with no less disapproval. 'And don't give lip to your elders, sonny!'

Paul drew himself up to his best approximation of maturity, which only succeeded in causing the man to choke back a laugh.

'No harm, young fella!' the man offered when he had recovered from his seizure of mirth, white beard wagging with each word. 'I'd be no sort of man if I allowed you to get hurt by things beyond your ken! Take advice well meant!'

The warmth of the tone soothed Paul some, and the sting to his pride eased.

'Who are you?' he asked, letting the man know that *he* was still in command of the situation.

The old man's eyes twinkled mischievously as he lowered himself to sit on a nearby breakwater.

'Ah, boy, but there's a question!' He fetched a pipe from his pocket.

Undeterred, Paul repeated the question. The old man lit the pipe and puffed at it conscientiously until it glowed, smoking like a chimney. Dinah drew close to her brother, anxious because of the strange man's silence - her parents had warned her of wicked men who did strange things to children. Paul stood fast, determined not to show the fear he felt, eager not to worry his sister.

'Lynn is the name . . .' the man said eventually. 'I used to be Mayor!' He smiled mysteriously. 'Now . . . I am just a fisherman. I own that boat over there - a fine vessel of good family. Many a voyage I've had with her . . .! Aye, 'The Dragon' is a good 'un!'

Paul's' heart was beating more slowly now.

'What do you know about the pollution?' he asked.

Lynn tapped his pipe out on a stone.

'Takes many forms, me lad!' He eyed the factory which stretched outlet pipes into the cove like plastic tentacles. 'Some look evil and give little bother, some are unseen yet quietly destroy!' He gazed seaward.

Dinah, more confident now, was quick to grasp his meaning.

'Ships?'

The wrinkled face smiled, creases joining. 'Aye, oil ships!'

Unwilling to be excluded, Paul added 'Tankers!'

The man smiled and winked. 'Yes, tankers!'

'They're nasty!' Dinah affirmed.

Paul nodded. 'People should stop it!'

The man's smile faded. He rose, slipping the pipe back into his pocket.
'Follow!'

Without looking back, he strode into the wiry brush covering the sandy soil just yards from the shore.

Oddly fearless, both Paul and Dinah tagged along, pushing through the knotty shrubs and into the denser wood beyond - something they had not noticed before. The ground grew more loamy as they entered, easier to walk upon.

Not far inside the man stood in a clearing, at the dead centre of which lay a huge rock. Sticking out of this was a beautiful broadsword, gleaming in the sunlight. At its side was a medium-sized wooden box, filled to the brim with jewels. Struggling for life in their midst was a small sapling.

'Gee!' Dinah said in a hushed tone, 'Just like Camelot!'

'Come, Paul Arthur Penn, make your choice!' The old man smiled encouragingly.

'Is that Excalibur?' Paul gasped.

Lynn laughed. 'God no, son! This is your future!'

'What am I supposed to do?'

Shaking his head sadly, the man replied, 'This is no legend Paul! You've seen the beach - it's up to you!'

Dinah and Paul gaped as Mayor Lynn disappeared.

NEAR BROCKENHURST
Jo Young

'I've told you before, I can't say exactly what time I'll be home!'
The last two words were drowned by the angry slamming of the front door, but she knew them by heart these past few months. She was confused by a mixture of emotions, relief that the shouting had stopped, and the sense of loss that always accompanied his departure. Had she been unreasonable, or had he started another row intentionally so that he could be out half the night again without attempting to justify it? She really didn't know. She felt she didn't know anything any longer except that each day brought its share of work and each night its share of tears.

The back door flew open and her eleven and twelve-year-old sons rushed in like a breath of fresh air.
'Hi Mum. Mum, can we have our pocket money today instead of tomorrow please? We want to get our PC magazine and the latest Steps single. Please!'
She smiled and nodded agreement. The boys hadn't expected such an easy victory and had come to understand that somehow this meant that their mother was preoccupied and unhappy. But the young are resilient and life must go on.
'Thanks Mum. Bye, won't be long.'

The door slammed again but this time eagerly and not angrily. As she filled the kettle, the phone rang. She answered it hesitantly, hoping that he was calling to say he would be home for dinner after all. It was her mother, however, the only person in the world who could read her like an open book.
'Would it be convenient if I popped round for ten minutes? I've got a little present for you.'
She didn't want to worry her mother and made an effort to sound bright.
'Sounds lovely. I'll postpone the tea until you arrive.'

The older woman appeared carrying a flat object in brown paper. She kissed her daughter and gave her hand an affectionate squeeze.
'I know you like it, so I decided that you should have it now and not wait for me to leave it to you!'
'But I couldn't possibly take it, Mum. It's Dad's watercolour and it means so much to you.'

The reply was unhesitating. 'I thought you'd been a bit down recently and hoped it might cheer you up. Your father would have wanted you to have it; he said he bought it because he could forget his problems when he looked into it.'

Suddenly the long suppressed tears flowed uncontrollably, and she poured forth the sad, the age-old story of the dying of a love affair. She felt disloyal somehow, yet immensely relieved. Her mother was, as ever, brief and to the point.
'Well, he's obviously got someone else.'

Through the hammering of her heart, she knew her mother was right; she had never known her to be wrong in matters of the heart. She heard herself reply in a thin, unconvincing voice that didn't belong to her.
'But I'm sure he'd tell me; we've always talked about everything.'

It was as though she had emerged from a fog, suddenly able to see things clearly. All the scenes, lies, absences, fell into place. It was the only possible explanation for the off-hand way he had been treating her, his lack of physical contact, his obvious resentment of home commitments. So the two women talked for an hour and by the time they parted with a hug, she felt calmly determined to confront him as soon as possible. But she also felt terribly alone; the house was silent, not even the comforting tick of a clock these days. All their clocks had been gifts and were digital. She suddenly hated digital clocks, computers with their impersonal faces, the video, the microwave, the self-timing this and that. What did any of them matter? She supposed he would be in his automatic car with electric windows, listening to the auto-reverse music system; *she* may even be sitting in it with him, no doubt with a digital face which clocks up other women's husbands. Does she know he has two sons? Does he tell her I'm evil-tempered, frigid and slovenly? Or does he avoid it all by playing a romantic CD?

She took up the watercolour and wandered into the lounge. She removed the Canaletto print from its pride of place and replaced it with the Victorian landscape. Normally she would have consulted with him; he liked the Canaletto and she had given it to him for their tenth anniversary. But today the act gave her a small feeling of revenge. Besides, the watercolour was an original and a print, Canaletto or otherwise, could not stand comparison.

She had often admired the painting in passing, but now looked at it closely. It wasn't very big, about fourteen inches by twelve, and was mounted on a gold surround in a gilt frame which set off to advantage the colours of early autumn. The main subject, towards the left, was a picturesque thatched cottage with a wooden fence. In the front garden rose a profusion of hollyhocks and sunflowers, and behind the cottage were two tall oaks in their autumn finery.

A dirt track skirted the front of the dwelling and curved towards the horizon, and there in front of the garden gate stood a woman feeding six chickens which pecked around her feet. She was dressed in the long clothing of the period, a white pinafore over her brown dress, and a white cap completely covering her head so that only a hint of dark hair showed above her forehead. The figure was just an inch tall and yet the detail was remarkable. To the left of the cottage garden was a four-bar gate of the kind that children love to swing on. To the right of the picture, in the distance, stood another cottage; the ground between appeared rough and was punctuated by gorse, and she could almost hear the high, tinkling notes of goldfinches. Seven birds were silhouetted in flight against the blue, pink and gold of the morning sky, and she guessed that they were geese. The signature in the bottom right-hand corner was written in brown and difficult to discern amidst the gold and brown grasses of that area. She rummaged in the bureau and found a magnifying glass.

'Harold Lawes, eighteen hundred and something.' Then slightly larger, almost printed, 'Near Brockenhurst.'

Brockenhurst. She felt sure she had been there in the past and tried to recall the place. Then she remembered the holiday they had had in the New Forest, she and her husband, before the boys arrived. An idyllic, loving, happy week during which they had stopped for tea in Brockenhurst. She felt the familiar constriction of her throat as she looked at the diminutive figure of the woman through a blur of tears.
'How I wish we could change places for a while,' she whispered.

The day dragged by and at eleven she gave up waiting and went to bed. She spent an hour tossing and turning, alternately angry and worried; suppose this time it was genuine and he was lying injured in a ditch somewhere. The phone rang just after midnight; startled, she gave the number hoarsely.

'Oh hi,' he began in a tone of forced casualness; 'look, I've had a few drinks and Bob's offered to put me up.'

Again she heard the thin, distant voice which didn't belong to her.

'Couldn't you get a cab?'

Where was her dignity, she wondered, even as she spoke.

'Not worth it really. I'll come home in the morning for a change of shirt. Sorry if I woke you.'

She put the phone down carefully without replying. How strange to apologise for waking me but not for breaking my heart she thought as she tiptoed downstairs. She made coffee with trembling hands and sat down opposite the painting, determined not to think about him. She thought about the artist, how old he had been when he painted it, had he known the woman? Most of all she wondered whether the cottage was still there; she couldn't remember the details of her visit. If it still existed it would probably be surrounded by new buildings; she felt a real stab of regret at the thought that it may have been demolished to make way for a road. She understood why her father had lost himself in the picture; had he wanted to know more about it as she now did? She was filled with longing to see the spot where the woman had stood; the scene appeared more real to her at this moment than the room in which she sat. She had enough insight to know that this was escapism, and enough common-sense to know that there was no escape. The day had to be faced.

No sooner had the boys left for school in the morning than she heard his key in the door. He looked pale and strained as he entered the kitchen, and neglected as men do when they need a shave. He kissed her on the forehead but she moved away and again spoke in a stranger's voice.

'Coffee?'

'Please.'

She filled the mugs as she struggled to regain the courage she had felt briefly the previous day. She set the coffee down on the table and sat opposite him.

He cleared his throat but said nothing and, fighting her mounting nervousness she sought to encourage him; anything to get it over with, she thought; I can't go on like this. She said just that;
'I can't go on like this.'

She had intended it to be a bald statement of fact, but something in her tone gave the phrase an air of great pathos. And then he wept, as she had done so many nights. He hadn't wanted to hurt her or the boys; this feeling for the other woman had been insidious but now he realised that he couldn't live without her. He had tried so hard but it was no good. She watched him closely and listened dry-eyed. Words of reproach sprang to her mind but not to her lips; they must remain friends for the sake of the children, and she was determined to keep her dignity. In her imagination she rose, walked to the dresser and, one by one, threw the plates at the wall with a resounding crash; but in reality she sat totally still, as still as the woman of the painting.

'And what will you say to your sons?' She was surprised by her calmness in the face of the truth.
'I haven't thought, I need time to think about it.'

She stood and went into the lounge and stopped by the picture. He joined her and followed her gaze.

'How long has that been there?'
Since yesterday; Mum gave it to us.'
'Nice of her. What did we have there before?'
She gave a slight smile.
'Only a print, nothing in particular.'

He came up behind her and placed his hands on her shoulders.
'It's not your fault; you've always done your best for us all.'

He meant to console but succeeded in patronising. Then the memory of another occasion returned unbidden; she was just ten years old and worrying about a maths test due the next day. Her father had come up in the same way and placed his large, comforting hands on her shoulders.
'No point in worrying, my girl. Do your best, that's all we ask of you. A hundred years from now no one will know or care whether you passed. Do your best and you need never be ashamed.'

He had been right, of course. Now she couldn't recall the result herself. And no doubt Time, the great healer, would one day put her present troubles in perspective.

She started as he spoke.
'I'll come home and talk to the boys this evening, shall I?'
'Yes, but please don't stay. No point in dragging it out.'
He looked pained and she was pleased.
'Well, I'll have to collect my gear at the weekend; can you make sure they're out so they don't get upset.'

Her eyes strayed back to the landscape.
'Just come when you like. I'll be taking them to visit a friend for the weekend.'

Her coolness came as a surprise and he sounded almost hurt.
'Oh fine. Where is this friend, in case I need to get in touch?'
'I haven't got the number handy; I'll leave it with Mum when I find it. We won't be going far, only to the new Forest, somewhere near Brockenhurst.'

THE STAR
H McLean

Esther settled back comfortably into the soft armchair in Helen and Edward Benson's living room and watched the young woman as she coped with the mysterious intricacies of the video recorder.

'I'm really excited to be seeing a film of your wedding.'
She smiled. 'It's one thing to be there but quite something else to see everything that was going on from other angles, so to speak.'
A few clicks and a whirr, and the blank screen of the television suddenly turned pale blue. Helen turned towards her grinning as the names of all those officiating at her wedding began to appear in quaint Old English lettering.
'Good so far isn't it?'
'It's fascinating Helen.'
And Esther meant it. The long shot of the church was superb, and the slow move across to the surrounding fields with the Welsh hills lying lazily purple in the afternoon sun, nothing short of breathtaking.

Back to the church again. A view of the gate where the guests were beginning to arrive. Yes: there she was in the first group walking down the path just behind her friends Margaret and Jack. A pity she could not really be seen from that angle she thought with a stab of disappointment, and immediately felt guilty. After all, it was the bride and groom's day, not hers.

Keeping her expression pleasant, Esther silently allowed her critical faculty complete and riotous freedom as she viewed the rest of the guests arriving. Of course, her side, the brides', all looked very good indeed, but she had expected nothing less. Her eldest daughter was Matron of Honour and her cute little grandson, Peter, a page boy who, thank goodness, knew how to behave himself on these occasions even though he was a little mischief at home.

Edward's relatives were a different matter. Good grief! Just look at his mother's dress! A navy patterned dowdy thing. Anyone could have been excused for thinking that she had kept it at the back of her wardrobe for years, and at least the bride's mother had possessed the good taste to wear a hat.

Edward was a nice boy, but a girl did tend to find herself married to her husband's family as well, and there was that bossy cousin of his to contend with. Ah yes; there was Ellen now, frowning as usual. Of course she was pregnant. Perhaps she had been feeling unwell most of the day; her sullen demeanour certainly suggested this.

A warm smile spread across Esther's face as the camera moved to the bridesmaid's car and she saw her daughter, Claire, getting out with little Peter. Exquisite! They were quite perfect. She had no time to look at the other bridesmaid, but it was only Edward's schoolgirl sister, Daphne, who could hardly be expected to hold a candle to a smart married woman of twenty-five, especially when she was accompanied by such an angel of a child.

They walked past the camera a trifle self-consciously, smiling then looking away quickly, and after they had stopped just inside the church door, the bride's car appeared, moving slowly and majestically, white ribbons streaming.

'I'll get some coffee if you like.' Helen offered, and Esther smiled vaguely as the girl slipped past her into the kitchen.

Oh what a feast for the eyes! Could there ever have been a more beautiful bride? Esther stared avidly at Helen, taking in her abundant black hair which, considering her parents' colouring, had always been a bit of a mystery until you recalled her late maternal grandmother's crowning glory. Strange how some traits skipped a generation like that.

'You look so lovely Helen.' She called into the kitchen happily. 'Come and see yourself.'
Helen laughed. 'Thanks. To be honest, I like watching it on my own but I feel a bit embarrassed in front of people.'

The wedding service was filmed from a point behind and to the right of the vicar, and Esther felt frustrated when it swung round to take in her side of the congregation. She was visible by only one shoulder, the rest of her being totally hidden by the lectern.

Helen returned with their coffee and they talked as the service progressed, Esther's eyes shifting back constantly to the screen. It was odd to watch this part of the wedding; the familiar part. She knew in advance exactly when Peter, tired of standing, was going to sit down in the nearest pew, and when someone across the aisle coughed too long and too loud.

The vows were solemn and moving and Esther felt thankful that she had not made her private nightmare come true by actually crying. That really would have been too humiliating.

The signing of the register followed the next hymn, and after a while the camera returned to the waiting congregation, and it was there that Esther saw her. She stiffened in disbelief, the smile fading from her face. The woman was rising to go into the vestry and she was anything but a credit to the bride. Dumpy and too short, even in those ridiculously high heels, she was walking with such exaggerated care that she might have been drunk! Her suit of pale lilac appeared absolutely garish on camera, and the matching hat with its net and back bow looked, frankly, silly. It was bobbing up and down now as she spoke to people on either side of her.
Heavens! Did the woman *never* stop talking?

A sudden close-up, and Esther flinched as the figure turned her face fully into the camera for an instant. It was hard to believe that woman was only fifty-three. She looked easily ten to twelve years older than that.

Helen was regarding her quizzically. 'What's wrong Mum? Haven't you enjoyed it?'

Dragging her gaze away from the screen Esther tried to smile again, but knew that the effort she made was pathetic.
'It's all beautiful Helen. Everyone looks so good, except . . . I just don't recognise that little fat old woman who's wearing my clothes.'

THE BIRTHDAY
Susanne Shalders

Hans' birthday. It is always hot on his birthday, a hot August day, making the candles burning before his photograph seem incongruous. Did he think of birthdays and August days as he lay gaunt and cold or was he by that time too numb both in mind and body? The photograph, in the flat greys of the 1940s shows a young man of nineteen or twenty scrubbed and polished in army uniform, his hair lifeless against his head. He is not looking at the camera but at a point to the left and is still and self-conscious in his pose. In the photograph the photographer's lights have bleached his complexion and give no indication of the colour of his eyes. The face is ordinary and expressionless, neither handsome nor ugly, and almost characterless for the lights seem to have bleached his feelings away also.

His sisters do not talk of him but they stop as they pass by and the sadness is there in their faces. Is it just for his death, the death of their only brother, or is it for the horror of it, the wrongness of it which caused so much distress to parents who had to live through other dreadful things too?

August, the month of Hiroshima and Japan's capitulation, the end at least on paper of all that had gone before but not an end to heartache. There had been other Augusts, the August of the liberation of Paris, the August of the fall of Kiev and that August, the August that began what would become a surrender in a Russian February. But long before that, on an early spring day, with crowds cheering for what was to come the journey towards that August was begun. Perhaps Hans and his sisters were there to greet and watch the spectacle that day in 1938 in the Heldenplatz in Vienna where the unity of two countries, long pledged by Germany's chancellor was physically embodied.

Operation Barbarossa. Named after the red-bearded Frederick Barbarossa. Forgetting perhaps, that this King of the Germans and Emperor of the Holy Roman Empire drowned in a river in Asia Minor on his way to Constantinople. His Third Crusade armies melting away to find their way homewards as best they might unwilling to stay and fight for a cause so far away. But eight centuries have passed and this is 1941.

The German sixth army is moving towards Kiev, one prong of the toasting fork that is also intended to spear Leningrad and Moscow. But the lessons of Napoleon's invasion of Russia are unlearned. There is no adequate clothing to keep out the Russian winter, no suitable transport for the rutted tracks that were the desperate way forward, the appalling tracks signposted by the broken-down armoured vehicles, useless in this terrain. Commandeered farm carts struggle onwards in a haste to reach some sort of shelter.

The photograph taken in 1942 had been evidence of an obsession. An obsession that was not manifesting itself. Already women wept for the very many fallen in battle who would not return but Hans' mother and sisters were not among them.

Stalingrad.

Stalingrad, strategically unimportant, but which must be taken and the River Volga closed. So much pride and two would-be emperors, hating one another, in conflict over a city with two names, one would-be emperor now in direct command of his army, the other knowing that he had time and that Russian winter. However, it is still August as the sixth army is sucked into Stalingrad. But its northern flank is ill-guarded and in four short days the Russian encirclement and a waiting as old as warfare. Debilitating hunger and cold would do the rest as the besiegers waited, harried, advanced and waited again knowing that the city could not be held, that supply lines would fail, that an obsession does not see reason. In that August it had not been difficult for Stalingrad to be reached for planes had protected and the aggressors were superior in numbers and tanks, yet making the mistake of failing to decimate the ferries on the Volga that would supply the besiegers. A weariness too was setting in and losses as the invaders inched forward into a horror of hand to hand fighting amongst the jagged ruins and smouldering fires of Stalingrad.

November. In Stalingrad the sixth army is completely encircled, in places doubly so, and in half a thousand square miles three hundred and thirty thousand men are on the defence. Then an attempt to relieve. Operation Saturn. Named perhaps, for its engirdling rings or even for the ancient god of agriculture ironies lost on commander Jan Paulus who listened to his would-be emperor. There would be no breakout no attempt to reach the advancing Panzer column, no attempt to save. Now the temperature is falling and the leaden Saturn looks down on 80,000 dying men. There is sickness and hunger for there is only horse meat, a little bread and a drop of fat to eat. But letters are still being written, last ones to loved ones from the many who knew what the end would be. They wrote even as they lay in the mud listening to the screams and groans of those outside the unheated hospital tent who could not be helped.

It is January and minus 30 Celsius. Men are dying as in a snowstorm, frozen, unburied and mutilated. On the fourth day of the month someone plays Beethoven in a side street off the Red Square the roar of guns unable to mar the beauty of the music or splinter the spiritual nourishment that it gives. Daily now the creeping loss of positions and knowledge that there was no future. There would be no more summers for so many, no more Augusts only this ghastly winter. There would be no returning to homes but death in a futile cause with the hurt of hunger and the spirit crushed into an unbelief.

Furniture for use as firewood is now running out and ammunition is in short supply. Those letters have left on the last plane. There will be no more letters or planes.

Are you still alive Hans as the final bitter fight begins? Are you there in the thirty-six square miles one of the 20,000 men still left? Sixteen days pass and you are not among the less than half who remain alive. Not there on the inevitable day of surrender when your commander, Jan Paulus, is elevated to the rank of Field Marshall by his would-be emperor.

The candle has diminished and is flickering. The photograph has shadows upon it now but the face is still clear and the eyes that will witness so much are unknowing. Soon the photograph will be put away until another August comes again, another hot day which will have no warmth for eyes that will see only pain, the hunger, the cold, and the despair. The sisters probably do not think of the emperor Frederick Barbarossa, he of the red beard, whom shadowy legend says did not drown in Asia but who sleeps cocooned in a cave until summoned by his country's need and whose fiery beard did not melt the Russian snows for another would-be emperor.

A FRENCH AFFAIR
F Jensen

The deep melodious sound of an organ soared out across the French countryside. The coachload of English visitors, members of the Orphean choir, heard it before the tall spire of the Basilica was even in sight. The choir was heading for Albert, the little town in Picardy whose name would be forever associated with the Great War of 1914 to 1918.

Then, British and Australian soldiers arrived at its busy railway station in their thousands to be kitted out, formed into units, given their orders and instructions and finally marched away along the old Roman road to the network of trenches some eight or ten miles away.

But to the choir members it was just a typical out-of-the-way French town. Surrounded by fields it linked half a dozen narrow roads and comprised a market square, a few unremarkable hotels, cafes and shops, and the Basilica - described in the programme as the Church of Notre-Dame-de-Brebiere - a majestic, imposing building, with the river Somme trickling beneath and a slender spire above, topped with a gilded figure of the Madonna holding aloft the Christ child.

During the war it had been shelled mercilessly and by 1915 had become a ruin, although miraculously the Madonna figure had remained intact, leaning forward precariously and still holding out the Christ child as if blessing those marching below on their way to war. What remained of the building had become a casualty clearing station, packed inside and out with wounded men waiting for or receiving medical attention or the Last Rites.

After the war the Basilica was rebuilt exactly as it had been. The architect's drawings had been preserved and it was painstakingly restored, brick by brick, to its former glory.

The coach driver slowed down as he rounded the bend. 'There it is,' he said, speaking over his shoulder to the members of the choir, pointing to the tall spire in the distance with its gold figure glinting in the sunshine. it was July and the choir was here to give a recital as part of the service to commemorate the Battle of the Somme.

Pam and Susan sat together on the coach. They were close friends and everyone knew it - the 'Two inseparables' they were called. Pam was dark, serious and quietly spoken. By comparison Susan was fair-haired, impetuous and outspoken. They complemented each other very well. The coach turned into the square and everyone was pleased to alight and stretch their limbs. By now the organ sound was deafening but, as if on cue, as they walked the few yards to the open door of the Basilica the noise ended abruptly. It left in its place a strange, powerful silence which even Susan hesitated to break. But break it she did. 'Wow! What an impressive place,' she said as they filed quietly inside.

David Hearst the choirmaster felt he should explain the arrangements one more time. 'The other events before us - the local choirs, the buglers, the service itself - will take up just over two hours, then it's our turn, so you see they're saving the best to the last. We've time for a short rehearsal before it all starts then we disappear for an hour or so before doing our stuff. It's an historic place so there's quite a bit to see if you're interested. Otherwise, there are places where you can just sit outside and drink coffee and watch the world go by. Just make sure you get back here on time.'

After the rehearsal, which Mr Hearst thought went off well, everyone wandered outside to find it had started to rain - a damp, chilling, drizzling Picardy rain. Pam was philosophical. 'Let's find somewhere under cover,' she said. ' I noticed there's a small museum across the road.' They both dashed across to the bay-windowed shop front, flanked by British and French flags and displaying wartime artefacts. The young curator, in hesitant English, invited them inside and stood back as they browsed around the musty interior.

Susan was quickly bored. 'I'm told there's a crypt under the Basilica. Shall we go and investigate?' Pam was strangely reluctant and seemed to be absorbed with the souvenir postcards. 'You go,' she said, 'I'll stay here for a while. I might buy something to take home. We can meet up in the cafe next door.' Susan tried to persuade her friend to accompany her but could see she was adamant. 'OK, I'll have a look around on my own. See you later. Don't forget we've got to be back well on time.'

The Curator watched with interest as Pam fingered the postcards. She handled them almost reverently he thought. Then she turned slowly as if waking from a dream. 'My great-grandfather was killed somewhere here in France,' she said thoughtfully. 'My mother told me that his body was never found but she thinks his name may be engraved on one of the large monuments amongst thousands of other names.' 'What was his name?' The young man asked. 'And do you happen to know which regiment he was in?' Pam thought for a moment. 'He was Thomas Layton, my mother's grandfather, and I think she said he was in the Royal Artillery.'

Susan had found the entrance to the crypt and followed the steps down into a large chamber from which a number of passages led outward. With one exception the passages were open and dimly lit. A single passage was closed by a stout wooden door from which hung a cast-iron handle. Susan could not resist trying the handle and found to her surprise that it opened easily. She hesitated briefly then stepped through into the dark interior. It was cold and clammy and suddenly she felt afraid. Turning around to retrace her steps she felt a rush of air and heard a metallic clang as the door closed. She fumbled for the handle in the dark, turned it and it came away in her hands. She was trapped.

Outside the cafe the chairs and tales were empty as the rain continued to fall. Inside, Pam sipped her coffee and waited for her friend. Her thoughts kept straying towards the small museum and its helpful curator. Other choir members came and went, surprised to see her sitting on her own. She glanced at the clock on the wall and realised it would soon be time to rejoin their colleagues. After waiting another ten minutes or so she left the cafe and made her way to the Basilica, the silver tones of massed bugles coming from within. She smiled and waved at friends gathering at the main entrance.

When Susan discovered she was trapped a wave of panic swept over her. She flung the useless handle away and shouted as loud as she could. Her voice echoed in the confined space and she kicked at the door, her shouts turning to screams and then to sobs. After what seemed an age she slowly regained her composure and slid to the floor to consider what to do next. Knowing that the passage must lead somewhere she turned her back on the door and began to feel her way along one of the walls. Her eyes were beginning to adjust to the darkness and she was able to see a few feet in front of her. After covering a short distance she heard the rattle and squeak of the door being opened slowly. A beam of light lit the passageway and she ran back, trying to summon up enough breath to shout. But then abruptly the light faded as the door was closed. Susan threw herself at the door, shouting and hammering with her fists, but she knew that any sounds she made were likely to be masked by the martial music from above.

Pam made her way to the crypt and walked down the steps to the main chamber. Uncertain of Susan's whereabouts she looked quickly down each of the passages. Noticing the wooden door she opened it and, glimpsing the dark uninviting interior, quickly closed it and began to walk away. Vaguely she became aware of a muffled cry for help. She turned back and opened the door again. Susan staggered out and fell into her arms.

They both hurried back to where David was assembling and briefing the choir. Apologising for their lateness they gave a brief explanation, hinting that the door handle in question needed attention.

When their turn came the choir gave what David described as one of their best performances ever. When they filed out to the coach the rain had stopped and it was now as warm outside as their reception had been inside. Their next stop was to be a certain restaurant in Arras for a well-earned meal before finally heading for home.

They settled comfortably in their seats, feeling relaxed and relishing a warm sense of achievement. Susan had finished giving the third account of her ordeal when she realised that Pam was quieter than usual and obviously deep in thought. 'What did you do?' she asked. 'Did you find a souvenir to take back?' Pam nodded and reached in her pocket. 'I bought this,' she said, handing Susan a postcard showing a picture of the Thiepval memorial. The photograph showed one side of the name-covered memorial. One name that was clearly visible was that of Lance-Bombardier T Layton RA. 'Mum will be pleased with this,' she said, 'I'm bringing great-grandfather home.'

THE GHOST CHASER
Nicola Grant

It had promised to be a beautiful morning when we had received the order to go over the top. The mists of dawn were clearing, the sun was shining and the pale blue sky had a few fluffy white clouds. Our position was on the edge of a wood. The sunlight filtered down through layers of leaves and dappled the ground. It was a day too perfect to be marred by injury or death.

I had the feeling that this would be my last day. It was not a combination of nerves, fear and apprehension. I had been through it before. This feeling was different. It was a type of calm acceptance of the inevitable.

We went over the top of the trench and into the churned up fields of no-man's-land. At least it was dry. There was no mud to contend with. Had my feeling been wrong, would I make it after all, I wondered. Then the machine gun had opened up on us. Comrades dropped down ahead of me either wounded or dead or else seeking the shelter of the ground. I dropped, blood pumping from the top of my leg.

I tried to reach my field dressing pack. If I could not stop the flow I would bleed to death lying in that field. I tried to move and a bullet whistled past my head. Breathing hard, I tried again and again. I narrowly missed total annihilation as something exploded inches away from me. This was it then. I was unable to move, unable to help myself or summon help from others. This was the last few minutes of my life. Unconsciousness would soon overtake me and I would be cheated out of my last sensations and experiences.

Just when I had given up hope he came. He ran over to me from behind keeping as low to the ground as possible. Bullets still whistled past me, shells still exploded but still he came to the rescue of one otherwise lost. Reaching me he crouched down on one knee and wrapped my field dressing over my wounded leg. He applied pressure to stem the flow of blood. I had expected him to vanish, leaving me there now that he had pulled me from the jaws of death. He lifted me as best he could. My right arm was over his shoulder and he clasped me around the waist. He almost dragged me back to the trench.

He laid me down very gently, in the most sheltered spot he could find, and smiled at me. He had such a kind face, fair hair and twinkling blue eyes.

'Lie still.' He said, 'I'll get help.' He turned to leave but I grabbed his arm.

'At least tell me your name, friend.'

'Thom Richards. Pray for me.'

With that Thom was gone, running along the trench. I lapsed into unconsciousness and the next thing I knew two stretcher bearers were standing over me and trying to move me.

'You're with us again are you, been chasing ghosts have we?' The man smiled as I was placed on the stretcher. 'Lucky your friend found us when he did.'

They carried me over the rough, broken ground. I felt every lurch and jolt. Bullets and shells were still finding their marks but now they were just noises in the far distance.

'Is Thom safe?' I asked concerned because he had not arrived back with the rescuers. Had he been injured whilst summoning help for me?

'I don't know lad. He told us where to find you and then he was off. If you know his surname I could make enquiries at the clearing station.'

'It's Richards. Thom Richards,' I replied. The man went quiet and looked in a strange way at this colleague.

'I didn't get much of a look at him. Can you describe him for me?' The stretcher bearer asked.

'He's a couple of inches taller than me. He's got fair hair and blue eyes.'

Again the strange look. 'I'll ask.'

I lapsed into unconsciousness again and remember nothing until I awoke in bed with a young doctor standing over me. I do not remember arriving at the casualty clearing station, the treatment I received or being moved to the place where I found myself. The stretcher bearers had gone.

'There are two officers waiting to speak to you.' The doctor said.

I tried to sit up but the effort was too great.

'Lie still lad. They'll see you as you are. It will only take a few minutes.'

The officers came forward. They were both older gentlemen in crisp, clean uniforms. They were the planners of war rather than combatants.

'I want you to tell us, as best you can, what happened to you and how you came to be here.'

'Yes sir,' I said and I began to relate the details of the attack and Thom's act of bravery.

'You are quite sure the man's name was Thom Richards?' The other officer asked. 'Is this the man?' He said showing me a photograph.

'No. It's nothing like him.'

'Can you describe him to me?'

'He's a bit taller than me. He's got blue eyes and fair hair. He's got a gentle voice with a southern accent.'

'Is this the man?' The first officer spoke again showing me another photograph.

'Yes sir, will he get a medal sir?'

'Had you ever met this man prior to today?'

'No sir.'

'Have you ever had cause to visit B Company?'

'No sir, I don't understand sir.'

'And this is definitely the man, you are sure?'

'Yes sir. He saved my life I would know him anywhere.'

'You are not to mention this to anyone. Is that understood soldier?'

'No sir, I don't understand sir. He saved my life, why can't I mention it. I think he deserves a medal. He could have been killed. The bullets were still flying when he dragged me back to the trench . . . '

My voice was raised.

'Calm yourself!' The doctor said trying to force me back onto the mattress. Despite my injuries I had raised myself up onto my elbows.

'Because the man is a ghost. He was shot for cowardice half an hour before your attack began this morning. He died protesting his innocence. He said he had become separated from the rest of the group whilst trying to help an injured comrade but he was found without his gun. The man he said he tried to help died without regaining consciousness and the court martial simply did not believe his account of events.' The officer who spoke was sweating now. His quiet composure was ruffled.

'I know what I saw sir. There must be an explanation. He is the man that saved me.' I said confused.

'I believe you. You're the second soldier he saved today.'
With that they left.

TELYNOR
Gordon Vale

This time, 'though, there was something different, something special cloying in the dusk air, akin both to love and dread, as once again she ascended the heavy slate path. It happened quite suddenly, as it always did, that, as she rounded a bend, all the noise below, all the huffing and the wheezing of man and machine died away and the grey of the stone was replaced by the greenness of hedged fields. A blackbird sang in the branches of a slender ash tree. The path under her feet still was hot through with rough and darkling slate which glistened now after the recent fall of rain, giving a deceptive appearance of treacherous, slippery scales. By now, however, she had trod this path to the old master's cottage enough times to feel at ease on the uneven surface.

The little row of cottages stood deserted with a crooked look of dereliction, like empty eye sockets, staring unblinkingly with unseeing gaze, yet with grim awareness of the girl's unhesitant approach. From none of those chimneys arose smoke, yet she well knew that the telynor would be sitting in the gloom within.

She stepped to the small, straight, undecorated door at the end of the row, but now she did pause. It stood ajar, which was no surprise whatsoever, for the master often left his home quite open to the elements and life beyond its walls. Yet something stayed her hand, some feeling or foreboding, mysterious and powerful and deep. Her hair and heart began to tingle and her breathing forced itself to silence, but she dared not glance behind her nor move her neck at all, lest any movement of hers break the web and penetrate the stillness. She edged forward, but the sensation grew and she apprehended now that it stemmed from within the cottage.

There was little light inside, for the old man had no need of it and only dimly could she see his figure seated at a stool. No sound rose and indeed his fingers at the harp strings were quite immobile.

'I've come,' she forced herself to whisper through the gathering momentum of that spell. At once, the feeling of invisible and magical breath, more potent than all the futile hubbub of the mines' machinery in the valley, vanished as though it never had pervaded. There, in front of her, squatted the solid, sane and homely hearth of stone and, near the corner, sat the old telynor. 'I didn't mean to startle you,' she added, aware that her coming had been uncommonly silent and that he had jumped a little.

He looked towards her voice and beckoned her closer, holding out the harp for her to take. 'I knew you were there,' said his lips. Confidently now, she grasped the instrument, lovingly drawing its poetry into her soul, for here was something about which she knew with all her spirit and being; but no sooner had she touched the beautiful frame than she felt again that strong and mystic awe with which the whole air seemed to be charged. A panic swept momentarily over her and her brow began to sweat with quite unreasonable fervour. Then, as nothing actually happened, she slowly started to regain control over herself, although she still had to wipe an inexplicable tear from her cheek before she was able to play.

As her fingers lingered luxuriantly across the arpeggios, she wondered profoundly if these sensations of invisible passion were familiar to the old master, for whom, of course, the whole world was invisible and had been since his distant youth. She glanced at the bard who was nodding with rare approval at her playing and she realised then that, wafted by the unseen waves of that curious presence in the atmosphere of the cottage, her muse had brushed briefly, imperceptibly, upon the inspirational. She was playing better than ever before; perhaps better than any harpist had ever played, excepting only the great old telynor himself.

Suddenly, a discordant spark pierced the kindled air about, as of a bullet on a calm lake, disturbing the dignified serenity of swans.

With a horror, she saw that a string had snapped.

Entranced both by the magic enchanting her and by the sudden ejection into her immediate and physical surroundings, she remained sitting transfixed, staring uncomprehendingly at the loosely twisted coils of that tattered carcass of a wire. It seemed almost an obscene defilement of the tranquil beauty of the harp's voice that it should lie there so bereft of life and song while all around that room strummed humming with the grace of rippling glissandi. For slowly she became aware that, in all that time, if time indeed had passed at all, her fingers had never ceased their plucking, suppling, coaxing at the harp. The old man motioned gently, but commandingly, for her to continue.

Then, all of a sudden, the breath shattered again.

It took her some time to appreciate that the second string had catapulted itself between the beautifully, perfectly curved willowing of the frame. Now her fingers stilled indeed and the music softened into silence. Yet that inexorable void began to grow and, as it intensified and brimmed the room full of its harmony, so the feeling dawned upon the pupil that her master knew acutely what was happening. A wan smile flickered over his filtered features and a nod of familiarity rocked his whole being into the slightest of movements. He looked, she thought, like a man who has long awaited this time although without, perhaps, ever quite knowing precisely how it would come.

He was now somehow a part of the peace and enchantment of the mist welling in every reach of that cottage.

'When the third string snaps,' he whispered liltingly, 'this old song shall end indeed,' but a stolen glance at the telynor told her that he spoke not of the piece she was playing, but of himself. A moment later, with a gruff, genial impatience, he added, 'Play; play on, see.'

Listlessly then did she take up again the instrument which was her all, her testimony and her witness, as it was her master's before her and she started a new, lyrical strain upon its surface and soon the fragrant incense of the music began to mingle with the strangely beauteous melody about her until she sensed that she had been spun soaringly into total harmony with the unspeakable mystery of love and dread which had so overwhelmed her sensibilities all evening.

She played and she played. And her soul wrought a song that taught of great, majestic age and told of pure, simple childhood rhythms of the earth and the sea, of the fierce primeval brightness of fire and of the thrill of the wind and the breeze in her face, cool and mighty, a draft from heaven. And finally, the harp sang with sure tranqility of stillness and she knew then that the old telynor plied his thoughts through her hands upon the harp. She did not mind. For this was how it should be at the last.

When the third string broke, a tear escaped from under her closed eyelids; but whether it was a drop of grief at loss, or of joy, of dread or of love, she could not ever say, not even in verse.

C U Later
Di Bagshawe

The up-river journey always seemed endless. Mind you, it was 400km door to door, or jetty to jetty. Sometimes we would go by road part of the way, that is the part of the way where a road existed. And existed is just about the word, it was referred to by the locals as the 'buffalo wallow' - huge holes about the width of the road, and with deep storm drains either side, often overgrown, so that there was no hope of avoiding the wallows. It was red laterite most of the way, except for one blissful stretch of tarmac the length of a local VIP's estate, and deluging tropical rain soon destroyed the surface. Every now and then the Roads Department would heave a shovel or two of muddy gravel in the vague direction of the worst holes. The locals had a word for this too, it was known as 'manuring the road' . . . so that the holes would grow bigger and better.

We were working up a tributary of the main river. As a highway it was rarely quiet. Each village had its landing stage with a waist high box on it, the public convenience. Beside which the women washed themselves, their children, their clothes and dishes, prepared their food and collected water for cooking it in. Not surprisingly frequent gastric epidemics broke out. The landing stage had to be a raft because of the rise and fall in the river, which when it really rained instead of the more or less daily downpour, rose and fell up to 18 feet. At flood times the villages, particularly on the outer bends, were awash. The houses were built on stilts and in the dry surrounded by rubbish, in which the chickens and pai dogs happily nosed, at least the sweeping floods acted as the Borough Cleansing Department. During the floods the people moved around by dug-out, and the dogs and chickens moved into the houses.

As the land route was pretty useless everything went by water. There were buses crammed to the gunwales with travellers and their luggage (including live items like chickens). Fish tail outboards on long thin boats zoomed up and down in a macho fashion, as did speedboats. As their wash destroyed the red mud banks and set the village rafts bobbing dangerously, it had been known for an exasperated villager to take a pot shot at the offenders.

Each village had general stores, workshops and coffee shops, so their provisions came up by barge as being too bulky for the bus. Great rusting hulks they were pulled by one or more launches. When the river was too low the shops emptied, and equally during flood times as the yawing barges were too dangerous to be towed. In between the mechanised water craft were dug-outs, carrying families and all their possessions from village to village, or to their smallholdings, or just across the river. Not being an aquatic minded animal by nature, having to crouch in one of these, nether regions awash and the tiny freeboard frighteningly near the water was one of my least favourite activities, though necessary at times.

At intervals there were fish traps where the river's abundant king prawns and their lesser cousins were stored, along with the great be-whiskered catfish, all of whom were a mainstay of our diet. Sadly I hear now that a Japanese cannery at the mouth of the river has all but denuded it.

Reaching our camp we passed the 'A' frame for log launching, on top of a corduroy of parallel logs set into the bank to avoid damaging it. Around the base a chain of logs wired together as the log pond, where rafts, vaguely boat shaped, were made up of sinkers and floaters to be towed down to the port, once the Forest Department had checked their royalty marks and girths. Beyond this the inevitable landing jetty/raft. Up the small rise to a half moon of houses behind an open space, these divided into 2 sets, one for non pork eaters, one for the pork lovers. The latter, being mainly ethnic Chinese, usually had vegetable gardens behind them, with formidable ditches and fences to try to keep out the wild pigs, and hopefully the monkeys. Each house was built on piles with a corrugated iron roof and a water butt each, normally rejected for the conviviality of the landing jetty and river water.

Behind these was the workshops, fronting the office, then the Dresser's Dispensary (he was trained in basic first aid etc), and going up a hill the senior staff houses. The office was air-conditioned by courtesy of fresh air, windows being opened on the side that the rain wasn't currently driving. Files were in cupboards with their legs standing in pots of kerosene to discourage the creepy-crawlies that wished to inwardly digest their contents. Communication, of sorts, was by radio telephone, static permitting.

The only entertainments to be found were decidedly dubious on the opposite bank in a small village. Otherwise there was the playing field used for a form of handball with a ball made of rattan, football, badminton and the occasional organised sports.

As can be imagined there was always a large crop of children!

Boredom sometimes brought on bouts of malingering. Some 'boys' led by a notorious rabble rouser, took several days off, then demanded sick notes from the Dresser. The leader was even suspected of at least one murder in the past, so the poor Dresser was too terrified to refuse. Eventually he plucked up courage to tell me what had happened. He was certainly not the bravest of men. On one occasion he asked me to go with him to a house where a sick baby had already been subjected to the attentions of a local 'healer' who wrapped him in leaves and did a spell or two. Prognosis was bad, he was completely dehydrated with gastro enteritis. At the house everyone that could fit in the room was crowded round the baby gasping on a mat on the floor, others blocked any hope of air in the windows. We cleared his mouth of rice boiled in condensed milk (at 3 months!) and tried a salt and glucose water, but too late. Hence the Dresser's stock was not high.

As soon as I heard of the sick note episode I sent for CU the ring-leader. He came from a Northern tribe who seemed to fall into two categories . . . very very good city fathers and Christians, or the complete opposite. He arrived wearing shorts and shirt and with a sarong draped over his shoulders. Like the Scottish plaid this combines the functions of coat, blanket and rainwear.

I asked CU for his version of the story, warning him that if it was true, by section XX of the Labour Laws I could dismiss him with pay just up to the date of his alleged sickness. He thumped both his fists on the desk separating us, then from the folds of his sarong drew a knife, gave a colourful version of my ancestry, then lunged . . . It was luckily a stout and wide desk, the fracas drew in others, so by the time I had got round the desk and through the gawpers CU was down the hill, thrown his knife into the river, and jumped into a boat.

With not a great deal of hope we reported the incident to the local police and the Labour Department, and life went on as before. However, one afternoon, the Chief of Police arrived in the office, as usually wearing side arms which he parked on the desk. Our Oz Engineer was with me trying to sort out sufficient bits of tractor to get a functioning one to re-make our road destroyed by illegal trucks.

One was always polite to the local VIPs, so the Police Chief was invited to sit and have a drink.
'Would you like to come across the river to the station this evening, a case of beer would be welcome?'
'Is it a sports meeting or an entertainment?' I asked.
'No!, we've caught your CU and thought you might enjoy watching us work him over.'
I became terribly blustering British and fair play, but the Oz Engineer escorted him politely out of the office congratulating him on the capture and made sure the requested case of beer went on the launch with him The Engineer's throw away humour had kept me on an even keel for years. This time he came back into the office, hitched himself onto the desk, scratched what was left of his hair under his disreputable jungle hat and remarked.
'You know, you've got to realise they've got no TV over there, you mustn't spoil their fun!'
After than I needed a beer too.

In due time the date for CU's trial came up in the equivalent of the up-river county town. Being a foreigner and uncertain of their inherited colonial judicial system, I was a bit apprehensive. I took my wife with me, at least she refused to stay behind. We clocked into the best hotel, suffice it to say I rarely complain about any accommodation now! The room was 'en suite', in that a cement wall about 6 feet high cut off one corner, in which was a showerhead with a limited supply of only cold water, a cement surround and hole took care of any water . . . and there was a squat type loo which my wife will never forget having got cramp in situ.

Early each morning I had to report to the court and left my wife to amuse herself as well as maybe, leaving with her my passport and some of the Mickey Mouse money, a suitcase to a simple transaction, a precaution in case I unwittingly infringed some convention and found myself behind bars, in which case she would rush off to the British Representative in the capital.

The court room was stifling despite some tired fans, and I had to sit on a low stool, straining to understand the 'high' language used by the lawyers. Every now and then the judge's gavel would rap, and I would realise that my legs had crossed themselves, a sign of great disrespect.

CU was looking subdued after his trial 'preparations' and was all too close to me. Our respective briefs gave long and impassioned speeches and eventually we were told that the next day the sentence would be given.

Outside the court my lawyer told me that CU would be found guilty.
'How long do you want him to spend in prison?'
'Surely that's a matter for the court to decide'
'Oh no! You will be paying for his incarceration!'
Feeling as if in a mad dream I contacted the firm's Head Office, there were phones there, and came to an agreement about lawyer's fees plus CU's B&B.

Again time passed, I felt happier knowing that a real trouble maker was well away from the workforce. We were all very busy as a short spell of good weather allowed us to work all hours possible to catch up on a previous bad period.

One morning there was a stir in the outer office. It was not unknown for itinerant pedlars to set up shop there, so I went to see what was going on.

There, completely unabashed was CU . . . my money or his sentence finished.
'What do you want here? I bellowed.
'Just come for my redundancy pay' CU grinned.

MY MOTHER THE HERO
Anthony Tamburro

As soon as I walked into the doctor's surgery, I had feared the worst - well you do don't you, what else can one think when you have just been told that you have a growth inside your abdomen? After dozens of scans and tests, countless needles and bruised arms, my worst fears were confirmed. *Cancer.* The word alone used to send a chill down my spine, now I was intimate with it, like a close friend. I had a choice: let the fear overwhelm me, or embrace it. I already looked like I was six months pregnant - I used to joke that it was my baby! Now I was being sent home to see out my final few months, or was it weeks?

It's good to be home, even if I'm not very mobile. This morning I made myself breakfast with a great deal of effort, just a wholemeal toast with butter and orange juice: food has lost all taste, it's just a question of eating to keep energy levels up. When I finished I realise how fast the seconds and minutes are flying past. I have never been so attached to life as I am now - too late, I laugh to myself. My son and husband are my greatest cause of sorrow and concern - leaving them behind in this cruel, greedy world. How I wanted to be a grandmother, how I wanted to see my son marry. Sometimes I catch him looking at me and I'm sure that he can see the terror in my eyes. Make no mistake, I may come across as resigned, almost calm, but I am so scared of dying, I am just not ready to depart this life; I have so many things I still want to do.

When I lie here in the dead of night, with just myself for company, I am overwhelmed with a constant flood of memories. Like the ebb and flow of the tide on the shore, they rush in and overwhelm my thoughts, tossing and tangling my emotions. When they retreat, all that remains is longing and regret. I'm tired, so tired, I know that I must let go. I wish that I could sleep, just for a little while.

* * *

I look at my mum and it is so difficult to comprehend why such a kind, gentle lady could ever merit such a terrible affliction. It has stripped her of everything; her mobility, her smile, her beauty, even her ability to eat or converse with others. She even shuns family and friends, a lady who loved the company of others. It is so difficult to keep saying that everything will be alright, when I know that she will not be with us much longer. I can see that the physical pain is not so much the problem, even though the tumour is now hampering her breathing and pressing on her stomach. Every time I look into her eyes, I can see the mental anguish, and I'm sure that every day a little bit of her soul drains away.

Some days I have to pinch myself, it's so hard to believe that this is happening. The year has been a blur; from when my mum first started complaining of stomach cramp in January, the news has just gradually got worse and worse. People say that it takes a crisis for one to notice the important things in life - how right they are. Possessions, careers, money all mean nothing when a person has been stripped down to the bare soul. This is the real test of a person. Even when my mum awoke after two weeks in intensive care after a major operation, her first words were - Are you OK, son. All that matters is how your loved ones and friends remember you. Were you a good person or bad? I know this sounds simplistic, but the soul is simple, it just becomes cluttered with the excess baggage of modern life. When my mum passes away, I know that she was loved by many and never hurt a soul in her life. Surely this is the most that a person can aspire to? I lie here next to her, comforted by these thoughts. I love her, but I want her anguish to be over.

* * *

Hope can be so cruel. It gives you that illusory glint of light at the end of the tunnel that keeps you in turmoil. When all hope is crushed, it is the same as when hope is fulfilled - the uncertainty is shattered and the absolute truth fills the void left by the enigma. I had been told that I would survive after the operation, and I can truly say that I reacted in the same way when, two weeks later I was told that the tumour had returned, more aggressive, more malignant, and that this time it would kill me. 'It's out to get me, I haven't got a choice,' were the only words that I could muster. Somehow, deep down I had known all along that I would not survive. You are your own best doctor and I simply did not feel right. I could literally feel the energy being sapped from my body from within. I have resigned myself to the inevitable, and all I want now is to see as much of my loved ones as possible, just to look at the energy and life burning from their eyes, just to make sure they are not suffering too much on my account. Leaving them behind is the hardest thing I'll ever have to do in my life.

* * *

When Mum said that she was not ready to die, I felt lowest of all, useless and insignificant. Even though I was doing all I could to help my mum, I could not make her better. It teaches one a lot about oneself, situations such as these. It makes you realise that you are not the master of your own destiny and that we are just here at the mercy of some all-powerful force that can take back the gift of life as easily as give it. The death of a parent can be overwhelming, but the important thing to remember is; were it up to me, my mum would not be dying. There can be no regrets afterwards, because the guilt will gnaw at you. You must try to fill your thoughts with the good memories.

When I look at old family photographs, I cannot comprehend the expressions on the faces of the people in the photos; smiles that will never be so carefree and complacent again, a frown when real troubles lurk in the future. My whole life behind me is being put into context by my mother's illness, and in so doing, is preparing me for the future. Even in death, the biggest influence in my life is still opening my eyes to many truths.

Strangely, I began thinking about how King Leonidas must have felt trapped behind his own walls at Thermopylae, staring out over the battlements at the Persian army massed in front of him, unable to move, beyond the fear of dying. How his heart must have soared when, resigned to dying for his blood line, he glimpsed the future victory of the Greek army at Platea and Salamis, just as a Persian scimitar completed his destiny.

* * *

Like the sun breaking from behind the clouds, a soothing calm sweeps over me, warming my brittle bones, soothing my heavy mind. I can still feel myself breathing, my heart pounding, but it seems distant and unimportant, like a faraway drumbeat. I've finally managed to get off to sleep. I feel alive with all this space to wander around in. In the distance I see and hear a woman calling my name; I instantly recognise her as my mum, even though I cannot yet see her face. As she approaches, I note that she is smiling and her face is radiant, almost ageless - 'Don't' worry my little one, I'm here now.' I feel myself rise from this broken shell, like a hand slipping from a glove, and now for the first time I can see my husband and son below me, bent over my inert body, crying. I go to speak, just to let them know that I am alright, but find that no sound leaves my mouth. At one point, my son looks up and I think that he has seen me, but then I realise that he cannot possibly see me. I turn around and take my mum's hand. Following her lead, we drift effortlessly into the benign, comforting light and in a split second I realise that we will all meet again very, very soon.

MEETING STRANGERS
David Barnett

Today was the perfect day for meeting strangers, or so Martin felt as he headed down to his favourite coffee shop, 'The Dome'. The heavens were chucking it down and frantic pedestrians hurried past one another - as though dodging umbrellas had become an Olympic sport and getting wet had become a criminal occupation. Record bag slung over shoulders, retro corduroy jacket with Adidas pumps, was all the protection Martin needed as he bounded along the busy West End streets. Hell the more it rained the more crowded the coffee shops - a thought that brought a smile to Martin's clean-shaven features.

Martin slicked his wet brown hair with the fingers of his right hand as his left hand pushed open the large glass door with 'Dome' splashed across in gold lettering. Familiar sounds of jazz, laughter and chatter welcomed him with a blast as he stepped over the threshold. 'Brilliant' he thought, an empty table had been vacated by the window with the perfect vantage point from which to observe the hoy-paloy that was cafe culture. One had options when sitting on the periphery; to observe or take action. The subtleties of social behaviour appeared to be at their height in such a setting and yet at the same time took on an irrelevance . . . people seemed freer here more liberated.

The misted window allowed no distraction from the outside world, heightening the sense of abstraction that Martin felt in his head; the feeling that he was separated from the rat-race in here - the demands, the commitments. In here the sole purpose was pleasure. Martin removed his damp jacket, allowing it to fall between the chair back and the small of his own back. Surveying the faces before him was immediately seductive as a kaleidoscope of colours exuded their appeal. To be exotic was not out of the ordinary here. A tall attractive, English waitress came up to Martin and asked him, 'Are you ready to order, Sir?' her voice all happy and chirpy.
'Oh sure, a cappuccino please.' Martin smiled in response.
'And anything to eat?' Her pen moved quickly across the small pad in her hand.
'Not for now, thanks.' Martin smiled again as she moved away.   -

Moments later the waitress appeared with a steaming hot cup of cappuccino and rested it carefully on the table.

'Thanks,' grinned Martin, sliding the saucer and cup closer.

'You're welcome.' Her smile was thankful.

Martin's eyes stayed with her as she walked back to the bar with her empty tray - she exchanged words with a male colleague who was himself smiling. One always felt part of something bigger when kind exchanges rippled through a crowd. Martin's eyes flickered onto a group of guys laughing and gesticulating just a few feet away from the bar; then onto a couple of girls who were intimately spooning cheesecake into each other's mouths. A mixed group of students could be heard on the table next to theirs, voices raised, as they debated some social anomaly or the other. Closer to home, Martin's eyes rested on the Latin American looking girl beside him. Her soft black curls gave way to the light sugar cane skin beneath it. Brightly painted lips contradicted a natural ease about her. The stranger's brow furrowed in concentration on the page before her. 'God and the Preacher' the cover read. Martin smiled, he hadn't read a novel for ages. He took a slurp of coffee, its bitter sweet aroma caressing his nostrils - it had hit the spot and now his senses were tingling.

'An interesting title,' he blurted out suddenly - on impulse. The girl smiled. 'Do you believe in God yourself?' Martin continued eager to begin conversation. His crisp South London accent gave nothing away of his Liverpudlian roots. The girl put her book down, sprawled on its front so as not to lose her page. Her eyes shone.

'Oh definitely . . . don't you?' she asked in response to the fog that had descended over his own eyes.

'Mmmm . . . 'fraid not,' he said hesitantly, 'I'm what you could call an atheist. I've never had any need to believe in anything other than myself.' The stranger let out a small chuckle, not in ridicule, just in knowing.

'Oh right, a belief in oneself does not have to be separate to a belief in God . . . in fact I believe that God is actually existing both within and outside of us. In finding ourselves we find God if you like.' Soft jazz continued to play in the background.

'I'm not sure I know what you're getting at.' Martin leaned in closer so as to lessen the physical gap between them.

'Oh please come sit here.' The girl patted a vacant chair at her table.

Quickly Martin gathered up his jacket and coffee. He clumped himself down before continuing.

'What do you mean when you say that in finding ourselves we find God?' His eyes were alert as he swept back a stray hair still damp from its earlier drenching.

'Well, look, let me put it this way, we all enter this world needing love yeah? Needing to give and receive it in many different forms. And in my experience there comes this discovery in loving yourself, in being yourself, that God is love. That she, well I say she because I'm female, but that God is creation itself, the universe, not the biblical view of this father figure looking down on us, but an energy that we connect with when we are ready.'

'So you're suggesting that we all discover God for ourselves then . . . it's not something that one learns from their parents or something like Sunday school . . .' Martin held onto the handle of his cup as if for grounding purposes, steam still floated off its surface.

'Well essentially, yes . . . I mean it's like sex I guess you can learn about it from books or whatever but until you are ready or willing to experience it, you don't know what it feels like for sure . . . you only know that something is possible . . . and I guess that preparation is all part of the process. I mean my parents always talked about God to me but never followed a particular religion, so my mind was never closed to the idea of a creator . . . do you know what I mean?' Martin nodded slowly taking time to digest what he had just heard. His eyes met intimately with this girl who was no longer a stranger. And yet having connected on a level so intimate, he still did not even know her name. Maybe she would have asked his by now if she wasn't so inextricably drawn to his spirit, on a level far less defined than that where names were common place.

They smiled at each other. Then Martin asked quietly, hesitant almost, 'Do you think we all find God eventually?' The girl continued smiling. 'Oh sure, it's inevitable really . . . even if it takes several lifetimes to do it. I mean there are people out there who are loving and kind people with no belief in God, but it's as though we see different parts of the whole as we go through life and then one day it's like - *Wow!* We are given a glimpse of the whole and then you know there is a God . . .

that's the best way I can describe it really.' Martin felt his mind leap as he bathed in the beauty of what she had said . . . felt somehow uplifted not just by what she said but by how she said it . . . this stranger who was no longer so strange . . .

'Hey can I buy you another drink?' Soft jazz wafted on the air.

THE PATCHWORK QUILT
Phyllis Spooner

Hannah carefully folded away the quilt. There was quite a way to go yet, but the squares were coming together nicely. She collected the various coloured threads and put them into her tin. 'Best to stop when one's eyes are tired, 'twould be a pity if any of the stitches were uneven.' There, she was talking to herself again. Where was Dorothy? She promised to call in tonight on her way back from the pictures.

Her daughter Dorothy breezed in about ten thirty and said she couldn't stop. Always in a hurry was Dorothy, she made Hannah feel quite giddy sometimes.
'I have to get Jack's supper, and I want to make sure that Catherine is back from the dance at the village hall.'
'Better get going then.'

Hannah was used to this. She knew her daughter had a lot to do with her full-time job, and she was grateful that Dorothy still found time to check on her once a day.

Of course, she could go to live with them if she wished, they had asked her to many times, but Hannah valued her independence and in any case she was only seventy-seven, that wasn't old these days was it? True her eyesight wasn't all that good, but once the quilt was safely finished, she wouldn't worry about that so much; maybe her eyesight would improve anyway.
'How is Catherine then? Still with that nice young Neil?'
'Oh yes, I think she's getting too serious about him though, she's not eighteen yet.'
'Well, you were only that age when you married.' Hannah reminded Dorothy.
'Yes, that was different though wasn't it? No one thought it would last, but we've surprised you all haven't we Mother?'

Hannah thought back to the hastily arranged marriage in nineteen thirty. Such a disgrace in those days. But they had survived it; Hannah had ignored the neighbours and was only concerned about the birth, and that Dorothy should have a healthy child. Jack had been very young too when they married, but he stood by her, and he had been a good son-in-law.

Later on, when Dorothy had gone home, Hannah searched through her pile of cut-out squares and found the blue satin piece which she had cut from her daughter's wedding dress. She recalled how Dorothy had been so unhappy at not having a white wedding, but had, in the end, looked quite lovely in pale blue. Then she searched for a delicate pink square from Catherine's Christening robe. There was a broderie-anglaise piece from one of the baby's pillow slips. Hannah smiled. She was looking now at a blue gingham piece. This was from Catherine's first school dress, and Hannah remembered the times she had met her from the school. She had held her little hand whilst Catherine had danced merrily along by her side.

Hannah looked at the unfinished quilt and a feeling of pride welled up within her. In her mind's eye she saw the finished creation which was to be her wedding present to Princess Elizabeth and Prince Philip. It was now September, and the Royal Wedding, the subject on everyone's lips, was to be on November the twentieth. She sat down and started sewing.
'Hello Gran,' called Catherine as she came bounding in a few days later. 'I've something to show you, look.'

She stretched out her left hand and Hannah sat down as she grasped the implications of a gleaming diamond ring on her granddaughter's finger.
'Aren't you a bit young to get engaged love? You should be having fun, not settling down at your age.'
'Oh Gran, please don't spoil it. Dad's already raised the roof.'
'Well, so long as you and Neil love each other it will be alright. I just want you to be happy.' She went on, 'Anyway, tell that young man of yours that I want to see him, I've only met him twice.'
'Yes, alright Gran. How's the quilt coming long? That's a lovely square, the green one.'
'That was a piece from my going-away dress after our wedding. Your grandad loved that dress. It had to last for several years mind you. Rob and I had very little money.'
'What about the royal blue satin? That's beautiful.'
'Oh, that was from the one and only evening dress I ever owned. The lady where I worked at the big house gave me that.'

Hannah's eyes grew misty as she remembered the night she first met Rob at the Christmas dance in the church hall. She had worn the blue dress and knew she looked good in it. If she was honest she was actually looking for a husband. Finding one's self still single at the age of twenty-three in the late eighteen hundreds was a bit worrying.
'Won't you be wishing you could keep this quilt when it's finished Gran?'

Catherine felt sorry for her. She had been working on this for weeks, and she looked so tired these days. She examined the neat feather stitching. It was almost perfect, and could not have been easy with Gran's eyesight.
'I know you're a royalist Gran, and this is all your idea, but I hope that the Princess and Philip will appreciate it.'
'It makes no difference Catherine, it's my work of love for the couple. She went on. 'I've followed the lives of the princesses since their birth. Did you know you were born the same month as Margaret?'

Catherine didn't know. She wasn't that interested, though she did admit she would probably see the newsreels at the cinema, if only to see the wedding gown. She would be taking quite an interest in wedding dresses now that she was engaged. She asked her grandmother if she had a white wedding.
'Yes, I wore a beautiful dress, have I never shown it to you?'
'No,' said Catherine, 'And I've never seen any photographs.'

Hannah told her that she would ask her father to fetch the box from the loft in a day or two. She needed it down anyway, but she couldn't bring herself to tell Catherine what she intended doing with the dress. It was going to be hard plucking up the courage to cut an eight inch square out of the beautiful skirt. This was to be the centre piece of the quilt. She would lovingly embroider it with the entwined initials of Elizabeth and Philip, just as Hannah's own mother had embroidered the initials of George the fifth and Mary his bride in eighteen ninety-three.

Now it was October and her task was almost done. Jack lifted down her wedding dress and Dorothy unwrapped it from its abundance of blue tissue paper.
'I just can't believe it mother, it's in perfect condition, not even yellowed at all.'

'The secret is in the blue paper Dorothy.'

Hannah hung the dress on the sitting room door to let out the creases. She stared at it and for a moment was back in the little village church of Good Easter, with Rob by her side. She wished that Jack and Dorothy would go home now. She wanted to be alone to savour the memories of that day, now so long ago. Besides she was now in a quandary. The more she gazed at her wedding dress the less she felt inclined to cut it up, even for the Princess. She put away the scissors. It would wait until tomorrow.

'Hello there,' Catherine bounded through the back door.'
'Where are you Gran? I've come to see your dress.'

It was Sunday. Hannah had read the newspapers, now she was resting before starting on her sewing.

'I thought you'd be round.' She smiles at Catherine. Each day she reminded Hannah more of herself at that age. Hannah had other grandchildren, two of them girls. Of course she loved them but Catherine was the one with whom she had a special affinity. She was about to tell her where the dress was hanging, but from the squeals of delight coming from the sitting room, she was aware that Catherine had already found it.

'Oh what a beauty, I've never seen a wedding dress like it.'

She took it over to the window where the sunlight glinted on the gold and silver threads of embroidery on the cream brocade.
'Would it fit me Gran? You were so tiny weren't you?'
'About your size I'd say. Try it on.'

It took ages to fasten the thirty or so tiny pearl buttons which finished at the slightly rolled collar. There were four petticoats which stiffened out the skirt. The dress was absolutely made for Catherine.
'Is there a veil Gran?'

Hannah had never seen such delight on the girl's face as now.
'No. There was, but I'm afraid that time wasn't quite so kind to that. It was so fragile and I rather ruined it by pinning on the orange blossom head-dress.'
'Never mind.' said Catherine, and her eyes were shining as she asked her grandmother if she could borrow the dress for her wedding day.

Hannah fell silent for a minute. No wonder she had been unable to take the scissors to it last night. And for what better reason?

'Catherine, it will be one the happiest days of my life seeing you at the altar wearing my dress. Take good care of it mind.'

'I'll have a circles of orange blossom as a head-dress then I really will look just like you on your wedding day.'

Hannah realised that for the fist time in ages she had sewn no squares that day, and what she wondered, could she use for the centre of the quilt? In bed that night it occurred to her that she could use a piece of the Christening robe which Dorothy had worn in nineteen twelve. Dorothy had declined to use it for Catherine and had now probably forgotten about it.

By November the first, the embroidered square was finished, the initials beautifully entwined in pink and blue. Dorothy came round to help with the lining of the completed quilt. She stared at the centre panel, then looked at Hannah who appeared quite embarrassed. There, surrounded by satin stitched pink rose buds were the initials of Catherine and Neil.

'What made you change your mind Mother? What about the Princess, and your trip to the palace next week with Jack?'

'Tell Jack I'm sorry.' Hannah ran her hands over the finished quilt. 'Jack will understand,' she said. 'It was after Catherine tried on the dress and asked to wear it for her big day, I couldn't let her down Dorothy.'

'She would have understood Mother.'

'Maybe,' said Hannah. 'But I couldn't put the Princess before my own grandchild.'

Hannah went on to explain how it had suddenly dawned on her that all their family events, the sad times as well as the joyous occasions were sewn into the quilt, a life story of at least three generations. It would mean nothing to the royal couple, but she knew Catherine would never part with it.

'I do wish the Princess and Prince Philip a long and happy life together.' She went on, 'I'm sure that if they knew about the quilt they would understand why I had to change my mind, and put my family first.'

'I'm sure they would Mother,' smiled Dorothy. 'Now let's have a cup of tea and start planning our family wedding.'

STRANGER ON A TRAIN
David Daniels

Only nine hours to go on the train. Nine hours! Never mind, he had books to read and, travelling through South West England had to be one of the most beautiful journeys to be experienced on this island.

Jeff settled comfortably in his seat, smiling expectantly at one of the books he'd brought to read: 'Writing For Children'.
'What's the book?' asked a chubby middle-aged man opposite.
'Oh, just a book on writing,' Jeff replied.
'Something I've always wanted to do, write. Oh, I've written a lot of papers for The Lancet - I'm a Professor of Neuroscience.'

The man was obviously proud of what he'd achieved, as the smirk playing around the corners of his mouth testified. Jeff noticed facial tell-tale signs almost unconsciously. He should have been a journalist, he thought - his mother always told him he was good at English and had an excellent eye for a good story.

'I could have loved that lady there.' The man had interrupted Jeff's thoughts and, for a moment caught Jeff off guard. He looked around at the nearest beauties, but no, it wasn't them.
'Ingrid Bergman,' the man assisted him with his bearings, 'beautiful woman and what a wonderful actress - always liked her.' Of course, the autobiography. Jeff was rarely dim but on this occasion he had to plead 'yeah'.
'Shame she died,' said Jeff helpfully, 'she created a bit of a scandal didn't she?'
'It wouldn't have attracted any attention these days. A tragedy.' The man appeared briefly lost in thought. 'David Norman,' the man said, offering a red blotched, overfed hand.
'Jeff Davidson,' was the monotone reply, a slim, long-fingered hand offered in return. The man's hand was clammy damp.
'Can't sleep,' Norman said seriously, 'read all the time at work so the only thing left to do when travelling is talk. Hope you don't mind.'
'No, no.' But he did. Anything for peace and quiet.
'Do you know how much my single ticket was from Penzance to Manchester?' Norman was going to tell him whether he liked it or not. His querying look encouraged the man to fire another fusillade of

words. 'Seventy-eight pounds! Bloody daylight robbery.' Just then the guard appeared in her fetching grey and red livery. 'Tickets from Penzance please,' she chimed.

'Do you know how much my single ticket cost me from Penzance to Manchester?' Norman looked accusingly at the helpless guard, 'seventy-eight bloody pounds!'

'Sounds a lot,' the guard said quietly, 'let me check my book and see if there's one cheaper.' She dug into her dog-eared tome, smiled and looking up said, 'I might be able to save you some -.' she stopped, her mouth twitching as she did the arithmetic. 'Sorry, no, that's wrong. The price is fine.'

Norman's face achieved a hue of the deepest puce.

'How would you like a cup of tea or coffee?' the guard tried expectantly.

'Oh the house?' Jeff tried.

'Yes of course,' the guard smiled.

'Rather have a price reduction,' Norman mumbled.

'Sorry,' said the guard, smiling at Jeff as she stamped his ticket.

Two minutes elapsed, during which Norman had started to tell Jeff all about his family, what he was doing in the South West and where he was going now. 'I wanted to stay down south with the family for the eclipse but I couldn't, have to attend a conference at the University,' Norman finished.

Wish you could have stayed there, Jeff thought.

'People think lecturers have long breaks you know, but we don't, we work nearly all year round. And the pay, thirty thousand pounds - it's not even an average wage these days.' Jeff grunted. Norman stopped and looked ahead. Another plan of attack seemed ready.

'My son, you know, is studying to become a lawyer: his first year, he didn't do a day's work, struggled to pass his exams. Suddenly though, he seems enlightened. Never see him at home, he's always locked in his room working. Marvellous.'

He probably wanted to get away from you, wise man, Jeff mused.

'Here you are.'

Jeff started. Just for a moment he thought of *The* Red Book and looked up reluctantly. Damn, just the guard. She handed the cups, spoons and napkins to Norman for distribution. He handed Jeff a cup, a little carton of milk, a stirrer and a napkin; the sugar was politely refused.

Norman was looking for more victims: diagonally across from him was a tall man in his twenties.
'David Norman, Professor of Neuroscience,' he said. Hands were shaken and the hapless man treated to a repeat of Norman's pocket life story, albeit with minor variations.

Jeff fell asleep. Better than Ovaltine, he thought, smirking. Jeff dreamed of hell, with Norman his cell-mate, complete with horned head, scaly tail and mitre. He awoke just as Norman was recounting, for the fifth time, the anecdote he'd first told Jeff five hours ago.

'Bye, then,' Norman said, shaking hands with all around him and handing out cards, 'feel free to drop in at any time. David Norman, Professor of Neuroscience.'

Expansive and attention-seeking in company, Norman seemed a small and lonely man as he walked out of the carriage and the occupants' lives forever.

The sighs around the carriage were clearly audible.

SCREAM TO THE DARKNESS
Paddy Jupp

'I don't want to come here!'
She sat on the edge of the chair trying hard not to cry. She would not give him that satisfaction.

Gwen was a small, dark child, just eleven years old, with black hair in bunches, her sallow skin pallid now with unhappiness. Her dark eyes brimmed with the tears she was trying to choke back.

'Why can't I stay with Grandpa and Grandma?'
'Because Grandma is not well and they cannot cope with you in the way,' answered her father. He stood with his back to her looking out of the large French doors that led into the walled garden.

Gwen could see some of it from where she was sitting and thought it looked like a prison. She hated her father and wondered if her mother knew that she was being sent here. She supposed not as she had not seen her for three years since that awful day of the quarrel. She could hear them shouting at each other now; her father hitting her mother and then taking Gwen away to live with her grandparents, where she had been very happy.

The room they were in now was very large, very cold and extremely dark. With no lights, the snow outside made it seem as though it were evening, although it was no later than two o'clock. Around two panelled oak walls ran a very large bookcase while the rest of the room was adorned with old paintings of old people. The inside of the school appeared as dreary as the outside had looked when they arrived.

Gwen grew gloomier by the minute.

The door swung open to reveal an amply proportioned woman, blouse drawn tightly against her large bosom, with a big green brooch pinned to the folds at the neck.

Her cold eyes swept over Gwen with distaste and focused on Gwen's father. 'So this is Gwen? Small, isn't she?'
They both moved down towards the far end of the room evidently discussing her.

Gwen sat on the edge of the chair nervously biting her lip. She watched fascinated, as Mrs Brand's ample bosom rose and fell with each breath and the keys at her waist jangled with the movements.

The door opened again and a young girl about Gwen's age entered the room.
'Gwen,' boomed Mrs Brand's voice, 'you will go with Helen. Take your bag with you, and that grubby handkerchief which you have left on that chair. Well, say goodbye to your father then.' Jangle, jangle went the keys as the bosom heaved and the fat body quivered.

Gwen picked up her bag and followed Helen out of the room completely ignoring both of them. If her father didn't want her then she could do without him too.

'*Gwen*' the voice boomed again and with more than a faint trace of irritation in it. 'Come back here and shut the door. Were you born in a field?'
Retracing her steps, Gwen pulled the heavy door shut seething with anger at them both. She knew she was going to hate it here.

Helen was waiting for her and as they went up the winding staircase, Gwen asked her how old she was.
'I shall be twelve in March. How old are you?'
'Twelve in four days' time, January 8th' answered Gwen. 'What a lovely birthday present, to come here.'

As they made their way along the corridor, Helen continued. 'It's horrible here. Mum said she would take me away when the summer term finished. I can't wait because old Pig Eyes is a beast. That's our name for Mrs Brand. You'll have to be careful of her. She'll punish you for the least thing. Come on, in here. This is your dorm, and your bed is the second from the end underneath the window.'
'Where's yours?' asked Gwen, as she surveyed the long room with beds along each side of it. 'I hope it's near mine.'
'Mine is in the corner out of the draught from the window. As you are the newest one I'm afraid you have got the worst bed. It gets jolly cold at night because old Pig Eyes insists on the window being left open.'
Gwen stared glumly at the bars running diagonally across it.

'Someone climbed out of that window about six months ago and that is when the bars were put up' said Helen. 'She jumped out and broke her ankle. Pig Eyes had her expelled. Mind you, that suited Janet down to the ground because she'd been trying to get away anyhow.'

Gwen put her bag on the bed, the tears rolling down her cheeks.
'Don't do that, she'll have a fit. Put the bag in a locker. You must never put anything on the bed,' said Helen anxiously. 'Do you want the lav?' she enquired. When Gwen nodded, she took her along to the end of the corridor where there were two white doors.

'In there, that one is ours,' pointing to the one on the left. 'The other one is the bathroom. There are two others downstairs but they are the senior girls' one and the teachers use the other. We're not allowed in them.'

When Gwen had washed, they went downstairs and along to the prep room. Helen opened the door and pushed Gwen through, whereupon she was confronted by a sea of faces. One girl giggled and nudged her friend, pointing at Gwen's bunches. Gwen shot her a venomous look and the girl turned away, shrugging her shoulders.

Suddenly a bell rang and the room emptied rapidly, the girls disappearing, chatting and giggling. Gwen looked enquiringly at Helen. 'Mealtime,' she said, 'but don't get too excited. You'll come out as hungry as you went in,' and she hurried after the others.

Gwen trailed miserably after her to a room which was pleasantly light after all the others she had seen. There were long tables stretching right down each side. The top one was occupied by Mrs Brand and the teachers.

Gwen sat down on the form next to Helen, staring at the two pieces of bread, butter and plum jam in front of her. She was still staring at them ten minutes later when she became aware of one of the teachers looking at her and smiling gently.

Nudging Helen, Gwen asked her what the teacher's name was.
'Miss Robinson and she teaches German. The best of a horrible bunch. She can be quite nice if she tries hard.'

Gwen looked at Miss Robinson's fair hair which was wound around her head like a halo, and thought how long it must be when it was loose. She smiled back quickly at the teacher, then looked down at her plate again.

The following weeks were a nightmare for Gwen. Whatever she did, she seemed to be in trouble. All the time, she seemed to hear Mrs Brand's voice. 'What are you doing girl?'

Everywhere Gwen went, she could hear the keys - jingle, jangle, jingle, jangle. 'Where is your uniform? Why hasn't your father bought it yet, girl?'
'I don't know, Mrs Brand.'
'Well, you had better write and tell your father that you will not be allowed out on the walks anymore until you have one. You will have detention instead. You are not going to show the school up any longer in that awful white coat, standing out like a sore thumb. The uniform is *green*' and she stalked away, wobbling all over.

Gwen looked after her with loathing, listening to those keys and wondering what they were for. She would find Helen and ask her.
'They are the keys to the kitchen cupboards. Old Pig Eyes doesn't trust the cook with the rations, so every morning she opens the cupboards and doles out the food for the day. Cook has to manage on that.'
'No wonder we only have bread and jam for tea; and it's always plum jam. I'm sick of it and always hungry too,' Gwen complained.
'So was I to start with, but you get used to it,' said Helen.

Gwen had become good friends with Helen since she had told her about her parents being divorced too. They both realised that they had been sent to boarding school out of the way of the step-parents.
'My step-sisters are allowed to stay at home,' said Gwen. 'It's not fair. I hate them all.'

Helen began rocking backwards and forwards on her chair. Gwen had come across her doing that a lot, only sometimes it was side to side instead. Often, her thumb went into her mouth as well. When Gwen had asked why she did it, Helen had replied that she didn't know, but that she felt better afterwards, and went on rocking, rocking, backwards and forwards. Gwen had become used to seeing her doing it now and didn't take any notice.

Stephanie was the only other girl who seemed at all willing to be friendly and she had a curious habit of hiding everything. She would put things under her mattress or in her shoes, inside socks, behind the locker. In fact anywhere she thought that they would not be found.

Nothing she hid was of any value. It could be a brightly coloured sweet paper, a piece of apple, string, a stone, anything she could find, but she got absolutely furious if anyone touched any of them.
'They're mine,' she would shout. 'Leave them alone,' and she would wade in with her skinny arms flailing and woe betide anyone who got in her way.

She would then retreat to the nearest corner with her treasure clasped tightly to her chest. One arm would go up over her spiky hair and move backwards as if stroking it.

Gwen felt sorry for her, so she and Helen took turns to 'look after her' and warned the other girls to leave her alone, earning themselves the names of Rag, Tag and Bobtail. They did not mind though if it meant that they were left to themselves.

Gwen's uniform had not yet arrived and she wrote another dispairing letter.
'Please Dad, send my uniform because I can't go out without it. Mrs Brand makes me stay in to detention all the time. Please send it *soon*,' the last work underlined heavily.

It was not until the end of February that the uniform appeared, but it was minus the green mackintosh.
'No Mac?' said Mrs Brand in shocked tones, 'No Mac? He doesn't think you can go out in that white coat does he? You'll spoil the uniform, I've told you again and again.'
Gwen looked down at her socks. They were white, so what was so bad about the coat?

She ran off to her favourite place behind the greenhouse which was at the end of the long wall in the garden. It was surrounded by high bushes and she could not be seen. Here, she squatted and broke her heart. All the hurt and anger poured out of her in great heaving gasps until she could cry no more. She felt better then.

Gwen would often disappear from classes, or the dormitory and come out here where she could be alone in her misery. She was not able to stay there for long though because it was so cold and when she went back, there were always more lines and detention waiting for her as a punishment.

Then a miracle occurred, or so it seemed to Gwen. She was allowed out for the 'Sunday walk'.

Standing with the other girls, wondering what had happened to change Mrs Brand's mind, she heard the dreaded booming. 'Come here Gwen.'
She went to the front where Mrs Brand was standing.
'Look at this girl, all of you. What does she look like?'
Titters from the girls.
'A white coat, I ask you. She spoils the entire crocodile, and shows up the school. Her father says he cannot afford to buy the mackintosh. Really!'
More titters.
'I knew it was a mistake taking you on here. This is a school with standards and I expect them to be upheld,' ranted Mrs Brand. 'Oh, for goodness sake get out of my sight, girl.'
Gwen marched back to her place with a look that defied anyone to laugh at her. 'I hate you all' she was muttering, over and over again, when she felt a hand on her arm. Looking up, she was startled to find Miss Robinson smiling at her.
'Courage,' she whispered, and stayed by Gwen's side as they walked to the park. She did not feel so alone now - perhaps Miss Robinson's plait was a halo after all? It was a shame she had left it so long to be nice, because Gwen had decided what she was going to do.

It began to snow heavily again. It seemed to Gwen that it had been snowing for weeks during that winter of 1946 and she was going to remember it for the rest of her life. Her misery up to now had been nothing compared to what was going to happen soon though, if only she had known.

The snowdrifts were piled up along the side of the road and around the park, in fact, there was snow as far as the eye could see.

Miss Robinson was out in front now and was pointing out to the girls the different species of trees or naming the various birds that were looking vainly for food. The ducks looked so funny as they landed, skidding, on the frozen pond that Gwen could not help laughing at them.

Gwen had been dropping back to the end of the crocodile as the other girls began flocking round Miss Robinson. Now most of the girls were ahead of her.

Miss Robinson turned round to hurry them up and Helen and Stephanie ran on ahead. Gwen bent down to do her shoelace up, then when she was sure no one was looking, she turned and ran towards the park gates, not stopping until she was through them and round the corner out of sight of them all.

Stopping some way down the road to get her breath, she wondered where to hide until the hue and cry had died down after they missed her. Then she remembered the old church which nestled in pine trees not far from the school and started running faster now that she knew what she was aiming for.

Suddenly, the snow gave way beneath her and she screamed as she fell headlong into the snowdrift. She was falling a long way and when she stopped, she could not breathe. There was snow all around her and on top of her. She struggled to get her arms up above her head but could only manage to raise one enough to brush some of the snow away from her nose and mouth so that she could breathe more easily.

It was so cold. Even in this bad weather, Mrs Brand insisted that all junior girls should wear white ankle socks so that they would all look the same and not 'spoil' the uniform. They were considered junior until they were thirteen much to Gwen's disgust.

Her teeth were chattering now and she was slowly freezing. 'Mum, Dad, Mum, Dad, where are you?' she said, over and over again, sobbing with terror.

Helen was fascinated with the biology Miss Robinson always explained when out on the walks. In fact, Miss Robinson had the happy knack of making everything seem so interesting that she always had difficulty in getting the girls to leave the park and go back to school when it was time, as it was now.

Helen looked round for Gwen but could not see her anywhere. She wasn't with Stephanie either as she could see the spiky head just below her gathering up lots of treasures to take back and hide.

'Miss Robinson, I can't find Gwen,' said Helen, pulling at the mistress's coat. 'We've looked all around, but she's not here.'

Miss Robinson sent all the girls rushing hither and yon trying to see if they could find Gwen, but to no avail.

Miss Robinson knew that she would be in big trouble when she confronted Mrs Brand with the news of the missing girl. Particularly as it was Gwen. Miss Robinson had been trying for some time to get Mrs Brand to relent and let Gwen come on the morning walks and this weekend, she had suddenly changed her mind, on one condition. Miss Robinson was entirely responsible for Gwen's conduct. That was the only way that Mrs Brand would agree to the suggestion.

Hurrying back to the school, Miss Robinson realised that this was the chance she had been waiting for.

After telephoning the police for help, the head girl was despatched to get Mrs Brand and to tell her what had happened. It was not long before that booming voice was heard above the uproar of the girls' excited voices. Miss Robinson screwed up her courage for what was about to come.

'I told you that girl was nothing but trouble and now look what has happened. You were entirely responsible for her and will take the entire blame, Miss Robinson. I washed my hands of any responsibility when I made my conditions clear to you this morning. It was against my better judgement to let her out on the walk and this has proved that I was right.'

'I think, Mrs Brand,' said Miss Robinson quietly, 'that you have been less than fair to Gwen since she came here. You knew that she was from a broken home and was very disturbed, yet you did nothing to help her.

In fact, you did just the reverse. You bullied her consistently. I watched you and longed to speak out, but I needed the money I earned to keep my father in the sanatorium. Now, I cannot stand aside any longer. Please accept my resignation as from now,' and with that, she turned on her heel, leaving Mrs Brand having apoplexy and the girls standing wide-eyed, not believing what they were hearing.

Miss Robinson stopped in her headlong flight long enough to tell the girls to come out again and help with the search, and they ran out into the snow chattering nine to the dozen about the turn of events.

Gwen was gradually slipping into unconsciousness. She was beyond feeling but her last drowsy thoughts were how pleased everyone would be now that she wouldn't be able to bother them anymore: everyone except her grandfather, that was. She knew he loved her because he was the only one that ever visited her. Come to think of it, he always brought a small gift from her grandmother, so perhaps she would be a little sad too.

Suddenly, there was daylight above her and she heard a man's voice shout 'Here, here she is, come quickly with those shovels,' then the sound of scraping as the shovels bit into the snow.

Gwen woke up in the sick bay to the sound of running water. As her eyes began to focus, she could see someone standing at the basin in front of her. It couldn't be true. She could see grey hair and brown spectacles and a little grey moustache. It *was* true! 'Grandpa,' she murmured.

She saw the joy on her grandfather's face and knew that everything was going to be alright now, because he was here. 'Oh Grandpa, I was so frightened, so frightened,' and she burst into tears.

Her grandfather cradled her in his arms and told her that he was taking her back to live with him so that she would have a home of her own again. Miss Robinson had told him what had been going on with Mrs Brand and what he was going to do to that woman was nobody's business.

'You can have your old bedroom and Grandma has found a delightful young lady to help in the house, so the three of us will be together again. It will be just like the old times. No more moving from pillar to post for you, my dear,' and he kissed the tip of her little snub nose.

'How did they find me?' Gwen asked. 'I was so sure that no one had seen me go.'

'Stephanie saw the red tassel of your school beret sticking out of the top of the snowdrift and it was she who called the men to come and look. She saved your life, my dear.'

Gwen could picture the poor little spiky head and see Stephanie catching sight of the tassel, thinking it was something pretty she could take back to hide. Thank goodness she had that passion for collecting things.

'Grandpa, you know the beautiful silver cross you gave me on my last birthday? The one I love more than anything? Well, would you mind if I gave it to Stephanie? She hasn't anything of her own to love and it would be a thank you present from me. Perhaps she would stop hiding things if she had something of her very own to treasure.'

'Of course I don't mind, my dear, that would be a lovely thing to do,' said Grandpa, turning his head away from her so that she shouldn't see his tears. He took his spectacles off and pretended to give them a good clean.

When, two days later, Gwen put the cross into Stephanie's hands and saw the emotions chasing each other across her little pinched face, she knew it was a picture that she would keep in her mind forever.

'You will come and see me, Stephanie, won't you?' pleaded Gwen.

Stephanie nodded her spiky head up and down, not taking her eyes off the cross in her hands.

Gwen smiled at her grandfather and he nodded in understanding. Next, Gwen hugged Helen tightly and they smiled at each other.

'I promise I will come and see you soon,' said Helen. 'Mum says she will bring me down in the school holidays.'

Helen had told Gwen in the sick bay that her mother had at last persuaded her step-father to have her at home and to Helen's surprise, he was coming down to get her at the end of term. 'Perhaps he's not as bad as I thought he was and we will be able to get along together after all,' beamed Helen and Gwen had thought to herself that perhaps it would put paid to Helen's constant rocking. She did hope so.

As she walked down the drive hand in hand with her grandfather, Gwen could not contain her impatience and snatching her hand away, she ran towards the waiting taxi.

Suddenly, she froze, for getting out of the red car parked behind the taxi was her father. Ignoring her, he ran up to Gwen's grandfather, and she listened in horror.
'She suddenly collapsed, Dad - rushed to hospital - died without regaining consciousness.'
Gwen heard the snatches of conversation in a daze.

Her grandfather's face turned ashen and as he took his son's arm, he was moaning 'Kitty, oh my Kitty,' and they both stood weeping in the drive completely oblivious of her.

Gwen screamed a loud, wailing scream. She knew the chances of happiness had gone with her grandmother's death.

She ran out of the gates, arms flung wide, head thrown back, all the time screaming, screaming.

Father and son stood with their arms around each other as her screams grew fainter, finally dying way in the stillness of the evening.

ELSIE MERRY'S CHRISTMAS
Ivy Squires

Elsie Merry awoke, eyeing the alarm clock she yawned then pressed down the button on top:- 'Eight o'clock - that'll stop your noise!' Having avoided its imminent clanging, the feeling of well-being, her long overdue decision had brought about remained intact.

Slowly coaxing herself from her cosy nestling place, and with well practised speed she simultaneously donned her mint green bathrobe, pausing briefly before the wardrobe mirror she exclaimed: - 'Make yourself presentable woman!'

The slim, five foot four auburn-haired rosy-cheeked reflection vanished into the bathroom. Ablutions over she again consulted her mirror image: 'Much better Elsie love - you'll have to do anyway!'

Feeling relaxed in a comfortable plum coloured dress, she directed her feet in burgundy fur-trimmed slippers downstairs, this first day of her Christmas break.

The fluttering of Christmas mail flopping to the hall floor preceded the metallic clink of a closing letterbox. Flicking through the handful of envelopes, Elsie recognised her sister-in-law's handwriting, she placed it to one side. Smiling with pleasure as she read aloud each greeting and placed them about the room; before opening the one from Amy she remarked: - 'You'll have to do it yourself this year Amy lass - I'm not coming!'

Elsie had been widowed in World War II when her husband's ship had been torpedoed and sank with all hands. Their honeymoon was his last leave.

The pain of remembering overwhelmed Elsie for many months, as she submitted to grief and depression. It was her reflection from the hall mirror that shocked Elsie's conscious thought one day, stirring her in spirit to rise gradually above her anguish. Her image bore no resemblance to the radiant smiling girl, linking the arm of a handsome young sailor in a black and white snapshot her Pete had commandeered a passer-by to take, outside the boarding house where their entire married life had been spent.

Elsie's battle to conquer depression was eventually replaced with a pride that remembering happier times encouraged. She took a job in a firm's canteen, driving herself to succeed and achieving the post of manageress.

Demobilisation occurred and rationing eased. Elsie remained single and was content to be so. She spent the following Christmas day at her brother Norman's house: - 'We must have her Amy - I'm her only relative!'

Amy was glad Norman had been firm regarding his sister's invitation. She had been very helpful and willing to share the preparation of the traditional festive repast.

Amy's parents and her brother and family always spent Christmas with them, Amy explained: - 'A well deserved break for my mother Elsie!'

As year followed year Amy's guest list grew and she herself spent less and less time in the kitchen, blatantly taking her sister-in-law's presence for granted. The last straw came when Elsie overheard Amy confide in her guests: - ' . . .yes I invite her for Norman's sake, she's his only relative!'

Amy's participation kitchenwise had long since ceased, now Elsie's fury escalated to intense resentment: - 'Well that's it - no more!'
For the time being though she would hold her peace, for Norman's sake.

Now the goodwill season was here again. Elsie replied to Amy's invitation with hypocritical intention. Then, taking a brisk walk to the mailbox she fed it her refusal: - 'That's that Elsie, well done!'

After expelling a pang of conscience she added: - 'Sorry Norm!'

Amy's reply was delivered on Christmas Eve. With a pang of guilt Elsie opened it, recovering as she read: - 'Dear Elsie Merry - Christmas, ha, ha . . . (Amy's annual joke prompted a fatigued smile as Elsie shook her head slowly from side to side) 'It won't offend me this year sister-in-law - ha, ha to you mi girl!'

Elsie read on: -

We've changed our plans too. I've booked Christmas dinner at the Duck And Partridge. Enjoy the day. Bye for now. Amy and Norman.
XXX
PS Maybe we can get back to normal next year, do you think?

Elsie crumpled the note and binned it, remarking: - 'And maybe we can't Amy dear - I think - not even for Norman's sake!'

A shrill 'Yoo hoo!' hailed Elsie as she rummaged through sale items in a town centre store . . . 'Season's greetings'
'Oh! Likewise!'
Elsie pretended not to notice the trace of sarcasm in Amy's tone, who then asked: -
'Looking for anything in particular?'
'Just hoping I find a bargain!'
'Well of course - we enjoyed our Christmas lunch - did you have a nice day?'
'Excellent - really enjoyed myself!'
'Oh! Where did you go then?'
'Helping out at a local children's home.'
'Working!' Amy exploded 'And you enjoyed it!'
'Helping - you'd never believe what a calming effect it had on me!'
Amy's expression urged Elsie to announce: - 'Must go!'

She hurried off feeling the need to hide a smile of satisfaction. For Norman's sake.

ILLUSION
Wilma Kenny

Jenny felt like a woolly jumper, lovingly knitted by a devoted Granny, squashed at the back of a drawer by an ungrateful teenager. No one would unravel her today as she huddled in the corner of the bedroom. She peeled the wallpaper with her ragged dirty nails, angry that her search this morning had not been successful - no hash, no booze, no tablets. She did not recognise her own image as she scraped the cheap glass in the mirror left by a previous tenant in the carefully constructed semi - a replica of all its neighbours. This tangled dull hair refused to glow of the russet colours in the sunlight as it once did. She would never wear those puke-stained jeans and T-shirt.

Jenny's nails dug into her forehead as she whiled away unpleasant thoughts - blood dripped onto her T-shirt from the dirty scratches she had forged. Like a broken dam that could no longer control the river's swell - thoughts rushed towards her. She yelled at the apparition. How she hated it when it spoke to her. She concentrated upon tearing the rose petal wallpaper, willing it to go.
'Jenny. Jenny,' it called to her softly. 'Why do you hate me?'
She squashed her ears against her wet hair, hoping this vision of her mother would fade away.

Charlie McGrath enjoyed a luxurious lifestyle. He mused on this thought as he made his way up the suburban street. After all it wasn't his fault if the houses which he owned, left to him by his uncle, were a last resort for those friggin' crackheads. Wasn't he a patient man - sometimes waiting months for his rent. The 'social' were often awkward - hadn't they tried to withhold rent from him after some junkie had been dead for a week. Dead or alive he still needed his rent. Charlie pulled his corduroy trousers up. Today he meant business. At other times they hung around his waist as he slithered up the street - hoping not to be noticed by the angry homeowners who would have gladly torn his dung-faced head from his cockroach-shaped shoulders for allowing dangerous riff-raff into the neighbourhood.

No 39 hadn't paid rent for months and if they had enough money for speed they had enough for rent. So up went the cords as Charlie marched like a newly-recruited policeman on his beat - or so Charlie thought. As he opened the gate the remains of half-eaten plastic-flavoured carry outs littered the path - and puke-coloured containers in which they had come lay where others had planted only the finest of shrubs. Charlie did not care - just so long as he got his rent. Fair's fair. He knew the bell hadn't worked for years at No 39 - Charlie wasn't quick with the repairs, so he knocked the door with his fist, only to find it was open.

'Can't even close a door - crackheads.'

He stood in the hall, driven by curiosity. He crept up the stairs, glad he had worn his sneakers. There it was again - a whining like a trapped cat or a small baby. He quickened his step - the damn thing was scratching his wallpaper. One thing Charlie hated was having to shell out for new wallpaper.

Jenny thought her body would never unwind. She felt her ears melt into her head, her hands ached from pressing them. She writhed, trying to dislodge the noise in her head - thump, thump. She now lifted off lumps of wallpaper - it just came away.

'Jenny, Jenny - it's Mummy'

Jenny gave in and answered 'You blamed me when he left, after I heard you fighting. I was only six, but I will never forget the putrid smell, night after night. I was only six - how could you have blamed me?'

'Jenny, Jenny - don't be cross with Mummy. It was all your fault, but Mummy forgives.'

The pain was unbearable, but it was taken over by something else - someone was looking at her. She jumped. It was him - that stench she would never forget. She ran to the dressing table and got the knife which Liz had left for safety - fearing a visit from a randy dealer. She watched him from the other side of the room as she had all those years ago.

Charlie McGrath was horrified. This was no animal. Blood was dripping from her forehead.

'Oh my dear. Who did this to you. Here let me help. It's OK.'

She was not unlike his own daughter safely tucked away in Halls of Residence as she enjoyed her first year at university. Jenny shivered uncontrollably as Charlie reached out his hand, all thoughts of rent forgotten.

'How did you find me?'

Jenny snarled like a trapped wolf. He came towards her but felt nothing as the knife was driven into his side. At first it felt tough but became easier as each time she pushed it in. She hesitated - for one second Jenny thought it was that sleazy rent man, not mother's old boyfriend. Yet another distortion. Suddenly she was clean - the pain had fallen from her.

Liza found her in the kitchen, adorned in red paint.

'Jenny, what the hell have you been doing. Oh no, you haven't painted one of the rooms.'

'Liza,' Jenny hugged her. 'I did it. I killed him.'

Liza pushed Jenny away realising that her new sweater was now covered in blood. Confused, she ran upstairs - there he was - Charlie McGrath, the rent man, was dead like a fox ripped to pieces by a finely-tuned beagle.

The policewoman was kind to Jenny. She had put her arms around her and stroked her hair. Jenny wept with joy - someone who would listen to her at last. She had waited fifteen years for this.

'Come on love. We'll get you cleaned up. Forensic will want your clothes - we'll find you something to change into.'

Police Constable Pearl Jones looked around the filthy room doubting that there would be anything nice there. Pearl said a quick prayer as she so often did.

'Please Jesus, help. Tell me what to say to her. Use me Lord.'

Jenny nodded - her face beamed. Yes, she would tell the nice policewoman all about it.

APOCALYPSE
Thomas Wignall

Have regard for thy covenant;
 for the dark places of the land are
 full of habitations of violence.

Psalms 74:20
(RSV)

London, England.
Present day.

'Oh Bugger!' cursed the elderly man as the number forty-seven drove past. He stood in anger as the passengers looked back at him in the street. He would have to wait for the next bus, or walk.

'What this world needs is a little war,' he thought to himself, 'something to shake up the miserable sods! Then they'll respect things a little more.'

'Ha!' laughed the bus driver as he drove past the moaning elderly man in the street. He brought the bus to a stop at the traffic lights and looked back at the old man, who seemed to be shouting at some boys on the other side of the road.
'Won't they ever stop moaning?' he thought to himself.

A businessman walked down the busy street on his way to the office. He looked around in the street and saw an elderly woman walking in front of him and an elderly man shouting to some boys behind him.
'Does nobody get along?' he thought as a light drop of rain touched his clean forehead.

The elderly man looked across the street and saw the elderly woman, a young businessman and some teenage boys messing around, offending a smaller boy.
'Hooligans!' he shouted, a sign of anger in his voice.

The boys looked back and an older one called back, 'Shut up you old git! Go off back home!'

'Kids today! Did nobody teach you to respect your elders! It's children like you that make my life miserable. Why can't yo . . .'

Before he could finish his sentence, a massive light filled up the street, blinding his vision. When the elderly man could see again, the elderly woman he had previously noticed was twenty metres in the air; the pavement where she had been standing torn apart. She fell to the floor with a dull crack and the man watched as a taxi landed from the air, right on top of her. The elderly man froze in terror as the lights tore up the buildings, cars and people around him. He did not see, nor hear the light heading straight for him.

Alex Bishop in his business clothes looked up towards the miserable rain clouds, just before he was to turn away he noticed a small white speckle getting bigger and bigger. He blinked twice to see if it was just an illusion but then it was even bigger, then he noticed hundreds more lights emerge from the dark clouds. He watched as one light finally hit the street ahead of him sending an elderly woman into the air, he looked across the street to see another 'light' hit an elderly man directly.

Bishop dived into the nearest shop and called across to the woman behind the counter.

'What the hell is going on?' he shouted as explosions and screams cried out in the street.

The woman froze as a blue saloon crashed through the window sending a child to the opposite wall. The woman behind the counter finally screamed as the building shook after another explosion.

'One must've hit this building! It's not safe here. Are you hiding here or coming with me?' he shouted.

The girl looked into Bishop's eyes but froze and didn't speak. He grabbed her hand impatiently and pulled her out of the shop, just before the ceiling caved in on the shop and the child. Bishop and the woman stood in the street and looked where to run, they looked right as they saw an explosion tear a bus apart, metal and glass thrown into the air.

A large shard of glass span off the explosion, slicing the arm of a teenage boy before he fell to the floor. The woman ran over to him trying to help; he looked at her and a tear formed in her eye.

Bishop interrupted, 'Look! He'll never survive. Let's just concentrate on getting ourselves out of here!' he paused for a second then asked, 'What's your name?'

'Cla, Claire!' she replied, a hint of nervousness in her voice.

'What the hell was that?' cried Fletcher the bus driver.

He looked back and saw an explosion rumble down the street. He froze in terror as cars and people were thrown into the air not far away. His own instincts made him run to the danger and help the casualties, just before a light hit his bus. He carried on running, ignoring the shards of glass and metal cutting up his back. Fletcher dived over the body of an old man and ignored the shard of glass narrowly missing his head as it hit a boy ahead. Fletcher dived into the nearest car and pulled out the dead driver, pieces of glass in his face; and he was surprised the car started considering the bonnet was smashed up. He drove forwards a little until he heard voices behind him.

'Drive for God's sake! Drive!' demanded Bishop.

'Quick!' cried Claire.

Fletcher looked back to see a man and woman had jumped in the back of the car. Fletcher put his foot down and the car shot forwards. Bishop was amazed at the man's driving skills as he skidded the car around the corner and manoeuvred it around other cars and the panicking public. But Fletcher wasn't quick enough to avoid a light that hit the side of the car. The explosion sent the car spinning in the air before it crashed down on top of a young man. Claire, Bishop and Fletcher crawled out of the overturned car almost unhurt.

'This way!' shouted Bishop as he pointed down a dark alley.

The three ran down the alley jumping over rubble and waste before they stopped when they heard a voice call.

'Hey! Down here! It's a lot safer underground.'

Bishop looked back to see a young man halfway out of a sewer man-hole. They all climbed down the long ladder cautiously and Fletcher slammed the cover shut as if sealing them from the terror above.

'Right, I'm Baz. I know my way around this place 'cos I work here. I know it like the back of my hand an' I've got keys for every door in this place.' he said as he flicked on his torch.

'What now?' asked Claire.

'Wait here till the explosions stop. Then we'll go up there and have a look.' replied Bishop.

'What the hell is that up there?' pleaded Fletcher.

'Missiles' replied Bishop.

'What?' asked Claire.

'Missiles. I was in the army for a while and there is no doubt about it that those were missiles!' he replied.

'But who the hell would want to attack us?' asked Claire.

'Russians,' interrupted Fletcher. 'Haven't you heard about it in the news lately? The Brits were threatening to launch an attack 'cos of all that business with those nuclear weapons.'

'And I guess they wanted to get us before we got them.' added Baz.

'Do you think the whole country was attacked?' asked Claire.

'God knows!' replied Baz.

The group carried on talking about themselves, trying to ignore the putrid stench of the raw sewage. They talked until the explosions had stopped, about themselves and what they did. When the terror had ended they climbed up the ladder to the surface. Bishop was glad to find the cover moveable, he worried that they would have been trapped in the sewers.

The group walked out into the street to see demolished building, dead bodies and piles of rubble. Claire hid her face in the arms of Bishop when she saw the bodies in the death-filled streets.

'Hey Claire, I know it's horrible but you're going to have to get used to it, okay?' he said to her, a tone of sympathy in his voice.

Bishop jumped to the sound of an engine starting, when he looked back he had noticed Fletcher had started up a large van. Bishop climbed in the passenger side while Baz and Claire climbed in the back and Fletcher put his foot down.

'Let's find somewhere to stay for the night, then we'll get out of here tomorrow, okay?' asked Bishop.

'Okay' replied Claire.

Fletcher drove the van around for half an hour through the devastated streets until Claire spotted a large hotel in good condition. The whole group stayed in a room together and later at night they got together to talk.

'Let's go and look for food, I'm starving,' said Baz.

'Half an hour,' replied Bishop.

'Okay but what sha . . .'

Before Baz could finish, a loud female scream cried out in the street outside. Bishop jumped up to the window and pulled back the curtain.

'What's going on?' shouted Baz.

Bishop stood gazing into the street, not say a word as gunshots echoed around the room.

'Bishop?' called Baz.

The rest ran up the window to see where the gunshots were coming from, they gazed in terror into the dark street. In the street lay the body of a young woman, her body full of bullet holes. Above her stood a soldier holding an automatic rifle, he looked back at another twenty soldiers, shouted and they moved on down the street.

'Who the hell are they?' asked Fletcher.

'Russian troops!' shouted Baz.

'Why?'

'They've come to finish us off for God's sake!'

A young soldier looked up at the peering group in the window, he shouted to the other troops and lifted up his rifle.

'Get down!' cried Bishop, as bullets smashed through the window and tore up the ceiling above them.

'C'mon let's get out of here!' cried Baz.

Everyone scrambled to the door as Bishop took one last glance outside, he saw all the troops running towards the front door. Baz, Fletcher, Claire and Bishop ran down a large corridor sprinting as fast as they could. The group ran out into a large balcony overlooking the main hall, large marble stairs leading to the floor from the balcony. They were halfway across the balcony when the troops burst in. Bishop felt the bullets whirr past his head as he heard the sound of the machine guns. Claire, Baz and Bishop dived behind the wall, hidden from the soldiers. But they looked back to see Fletcher be shot in the lower leg by a flying bullet. The impact sent him spinning down the stairs as he screamed in pain from the wound. Then there was silence.

'Come out with your hands up!' Bishop heard a foreign voice call as he gasped for air. The call sounded very poor English, Bishop heard the 'up' sounded more like 'ap' and the 'with' sounded like 'vith'.

'You have three seconds . . . or your comrade gets it!' the soldier called.

'Run!' called the injured Fletcher.

Bishop took a quick glance around the corner, Fletcher was on his knees despite his injury and a soldier held a rifle pressing hard against his head.

'One . . .' called the soldier.

Bishop's mind was clogged with ideas of what to do. Would they kill him and Fletcher?

'. . . Two . . .'

Bishop turned to Baz 'They'll kill us if we go out!'

'But what about Fletcher?' replied Baz.

'. . . Three!'

'Okay, we'll come out!' cried Bishop as he jumped from behind the wall.

'Ha . . .' laughed the soldier 'too late!'

Bishop cried out as the soldier shot Fletcher straight through the head, Fletcher's limp body fell to the ground as blood spilled from his head. The soldiers aimed their rifles up towards Bishop, he jumped back as bullets thudded into the wall where he was standing. He turned to see Baz and Claire at the other end of the corridor, he ran as fast as he could, but he still felt like he was running too slowly. They ran into a small hotel room only to see the opposite wall had been blown away by missiles. Bishop ran over and looked down, it was way too far from someone to jump down. He looked to his right to see a long iron drainpipe running down the side of the building. He jumped out and grabbed on to it, he then slid down the pipe until he reached the ground. Baz followed and the two men looked up to the frozen Claire.

'C'mon!' Baz screamed.

'I can't!' she shouted back.

Just then the soldiers burst into the room, Claire leapt from the floor and fell towards the ground, to be caught in the arms of Baz. The soldiers looked down and began to fire their rifles at the running three. They ran out into a demolished street only to see an armed guard with his back to them in the dark.

'What now?' whispered Claire.

'There's an entrance to the subway round the corner.' replied Baz.

'Wait a minute!' whispered Bishop.

He picked up a house brick from the floor and slowly crept towards the soldier, he lifted the brick high in the air and slammed it on the soldier's head. He dropped to the floor and Bishop picked up his gun.

'Right, let's go' he called.

Bishop, Baz and Claire moved through the streets carefully, avoiding the troops on the lookout. When they reached the subway entrance they stopped.

Bishop looked down the long stairs into the darkness. 'Something's not right! This is too easy!'

Just as he said that, a green jeep burst out from around a corner, before skidding to a halt.

'Go!' cried Bishop 'I'll hold 'em off!'

Baz and Claire sprinted down the endless stairs as Bishop lifted his rifle. He let off a burst of bullets from it as he walked backwards, feeling the recoil of the gun. The first few shots missed the soldiers as their bullets soared past his head. Then he took a deep breath and aimed again, he fired and the bullets thudded into a soldier by the left of the jeep. His body was sent flying backwards from the impact, his chest covered in blood. Bishop looked to the right and fired at another soldier, hitting him in the face. He was about to fire at the last soldier when he stumbled over a corpse and was sent rolling down the stairs, into the darkness of the subway. He felt each step press into his body as the world around him became a blur. Then darkness . . .

Bishop opened his eyes and looked around him, just darkness.

'Bishop?' he heard Baz call.

'Wh, what? Why can't I see?' he asked.

'We're in the tunnel, it's too dark to see' he replied.

Bishop stood up and saw the faint shapes of Baz and Claire.

'What happened?' asked Bishop.

'You fell down those steps and landed right in front of me!' he replied. 'So I picked you up and we ran down the tunnel.'

'Did you get the gun?' Bishop asked.

'No, you must've dropped it at the top.' added Claire.

'So where are the soldiers then?' asked Bishop.

'Damn! They're here!' shouted Baz.

Bishop looked into the distance and saw the silhouettes of many soldiers running down the tunnel. Then he looked in the other direction and saw soldiers at the other end. Baz moved over to the wall and leant against it.

'We're trapped!'

Just after he said that, the felt a strong metal pipe sticking out of the wall, he pushed it down and the wall moved. He fell backwards and shouted to the others.

'In here!' called Baz as he looked for his torch. He flicked it on and realised what he thought was a metal pipe was really a door handle, and when the wall moved, it was a door. Bishop leant against it and flicked the lock across, Claire flicked the light on as the iron door began to rumble. Baz joined Bishop at the door, reinforcing it as the door vibrated from the soldiers. Claire looked around and saw a few cupboards, a table and chairs, a large grate in the floor and a door opposite them with the mark G4.

'I know where we are! Claire take this key and open that door with G4, hurry up this door won't hold much longer!' cried Baz.

'How do you know?' she replied.

'Don't forget I work under here!'

She ran across the room and screamed when a gunshot rang around the room, the keys slipped from her hands and slowly dropped down the grate.

'Damn Claire! Can you get your hand down?' as the door vibrated from the gunshots.

She carefully slid her hand through the tight gap stretching for the keys, then slowly she let her arm progress further and further down until she couldn't reach any further, her fingers lightly touching the keys.

'I can't reach!' she cried.

'Claire! Those keys are our only way out! We can't hold this door for much longer, these guys are going to burst in! Hurry!' shouted Bishop.

Claire pushed her arm as hard as she could until she screamed, something had dug deep into her hand. Bishop left the door to see why she was wailing. He looked to see a large bulldog with its teeth dug deep into her hand.

'Pull your hand out!' shouted Bishop.

She pulled as hard as she could but the bulldog refused to let go, keeping her stuck. The door shook as more soldiers smashed it in.

'It's gonna go any minute!' cried Baz.

Claire looked up and pointed to an axe on the table with her other hand. Bishop ran over and grabbed it.

'Are you sure?' asked Bishop.

'Use it quick!' she screamed in pain. Her hand being torn apart.

He lifted the axe into the air.

'Ready?' he called.

He gripped the axe tighter. She looked into his eyes. He saw the dog's teeth. He looked at the target. Bishop waited . . . frozen.

'C'mon!' screamed Baz as the bolts on the door fell apart.

Bishop brought the axe straight down on her wrist and watched as the bone and flesh tore apart. She fell back and screamed in pain as crimson blood gushed from her wrist, pouring onto her clothes. Bishop tore off his shirt and wrapped it round the wound and used his tie to keep it in place. Claire sat crying and shaking from the shock, Bishop looked down the grate and the dog was gone; at the bottom laid the keys, covered in blood, the hand gone.

'There's no way out of here!' shouted Baz, 'Those keys opened the other door!'

'Hold that door, I have an idea!' shouted Bishop. The tension building even more on the other side of the doors. Baz was trying his best but the door was beginning to give way.

Bishop ran over to the G4 door and leant the axe against it, Claire and Baz gazed at him wondering what the hell he was doing. Bishop lifted up his foot and smashed the handle in half. He picked up one half and inserted into the G4 lock and turned. The lock loosened with a slow scraping and Bishop opened the door. Claire and Bishop ran through and looked back at Baz, he left the door he was holding and ran for the G4 door. He heard the door give way behind him and Bishop slammed the G4 door shut. He slid the piece of axe in the lock, turned it, locking it; and snapped of the wood making the door unopenable with the wood inside.

'That should hold 'em!' he said as he heard Russian voices curse from the other side.

They looked forwards and found themselves in a small dark room, in front of them was a ladder leading straight up.

'This'll lead to the surface!' said Baz.

They climbed up, Claire moaned as she struggled to climb behind them. Baz climbed out and realised he was in familiar place, a demolished Downing Street. He climbed out and jumped when he felt shouting in his ear, he had just climbed out in front of a soldier. The soldier lifted his rifle into Baz's face and pressed against his cheek, Baz watched as the soldier's finger curled round the trigger. From below, Bishop grabbed the soldier's ankle distracting him, Baz grabbed the gun, turned it back in the soldier's face and blasted him in the face. Blood spurted into Baz's face as his limp body fell back to the ground. Bishop pulled Claire up and he ran over to a jeep and jumped into the driver's seat.

'Damn! No keys!' cursed Bishop.

'Here,' called Baz as he threw the keys, 'the soldier had 'em!'

Bishop slid in the key and started up the jeep with a roar.

Claire climbed in the passenger side and Baz jumped in the back. Bishop looked at Claire who sat sobering, he worried if the loss of blood would not kill her. But he refused to say anything, more shock would be the last thing she would need now.

'Here,' Baz interrupted, 'there's a few guns here!'

He handed Bishop and automatic similar to his own and handed Claire a small pistol.

'Do you think you can use it?' Baz asked.

'I suppose' she replied.

Bishop drove straight forwards and then when he thought there were no soldiers he turned left, straight in front of a group of Russians.

'Damn!' he cursed.

He looked ahead and saw seven soldiers with their rifles pointed straight for the jeep, behind them were two tanks with the cannons aimed directly at them.

'Why aren't they shooting?' said Claire as she gazed ahead.

'Dunno . . .' replied Bishop.

'Put your hands in the air!' called a familiar voice.

They looked back and saw the man who had executed Fletcher back at the hotel.

'So we meet again!' called the man.

'Who are you?' asked Baz.

'General Ouromov' he replied. 'I can't say it's a pleasure to meet you!' he said sarcastically. 'Now . . . get out of the jeep!'

Claire looked back and saw Ouromov sat in a jeep with three soldiers stood by it, holding rifles. She turned forwards and her knee nudged the glove compartment in front of her, and out fell a small grenade which landed on the floor of the jeep. She slowly picked it up and nudged Bishop, he looked and a smile grew on his face. She pulled out the pin and the grenade began to vibrate, Bishop stood up and began distracting the soldiers.

'Hey, why kill us! What have we done to you!' he called, the soldiers stared at him.

Claire hung her arm out of the jeep and rolled the grenade into the centre of the soldiers ahead of them. Bishop sat down and began to laugh, the soldiers stared at him curiously. The grenade exploded and sent the guards high into the air, Baz looked up and saw a guard soar over his head, screaming before he hit the ground head first. Bishop sped the jeep through the smoke, behind he could hear the roar of Ouromov's jeep and bullets thudding into the back of the jeep, narrowly missing them. Bishop guided the jeep through the debris and sped forwards, Baz looked back and saw Ouromov metres away from them.

Bishop drove the jeep through the streets until they reached the motorway. He looked back and saw Ouromov still on their tail.

'Won't he ever give up?' pleaded Baz.

The jeep sped forwards while dodging through piles of cars, then Bishop felt a bullet whirr past his head. He looked back to see Ouromov driving one-handed, whilst holding a pistol in his other hand. Baz turned back and aimed the rifle at Ouromov, he fired but Ouromov swerved and the bullets missed.

Ouromov raised his gun and fired back.

'Baz?' asked Bishop.

No reply.

'Baz!' he repeated.

Bishop looked over his shoulder and saw Baz leant against the side of the jeep, eyes closed, bullet holes in his chest.

'Damn!' cursed Bishop.

Claire looked back and stared at Baz's limp body, until she noticed Ouromov had gone.

'Where's Ouromov?' she asked.

Bishop looked to his right to see the general had drove alongside them, Bishop lifted his gun but Ouromov slammed into the side of them causing Bishop to drop his gun into the road. Then Ouromov slammed his foot down and sped ahead of Bishop and Claire, by now they were dodging between the rubble at over one hundred miles per hour and Bishop concentrated as hard as he could as the road shot by.

'What's he doing?' asked Claire as Ouromov moved his jeep directly in front of them.

At that moment he slammed on his brakes and Bishop smashed into the back of Ouromov. The jeeps were sent spiralling into the air, Claire grabbed the dashboard as Bishop shot out of the vehicle, soaring through the air. He thudded down onto the ground rolling over and over on the loose tarmac. He opened his eyes when there was silence, he stared into the sky.

'Help me!' screamed Claire.

He sat up and looked at her, her legs trapped underneath the ruined jeep she sat in moments ago. Bishop ran over and grabbed her arm, but she wouldn't move.

Claire looked at him, 'Bishop? Is Ouromov . . .?'

Bishop looked back and stared at the smashed up jeep Ouromov had been driving. Then he stumbled from behind it and lifted up the gun in his bloodied hand.

'Time . . . to . . . die!' Ouromov screamed.

The hammer of his gun clicked repeatedly, the gun was empty of ammo. Bishop stood frozen.

'No . . . Ouromov,' replied Claire from under the jeep, 'time for you to die!'

She fired the gun, the bullets smashing into his forehead, his limp body was sent to the ground with a thud.

Bishop grabbed Claire's arm and pulled with the energy he had left. Slowly she moved from under the wreckage and climbed to her feet.

'I suppose this is the end!' said Claire. 'We got away!'

'It can't be the end,' he replied, 'what about all the other cities!'

'At least we're still alive!' Claire added.

'I guess!'

Many people had died in the chaos in the city the day before. What mankind is capable of can bring joy and happiness to people, but the technology of mankind creates the opposite.

Bishop turned to Claire, 'This isn't the end! Those damn Russians are still out there and they've taken many people from us. And I ain't gonna stop till I have my revenge!'

The survivors walked away into the distance as the morning sun rose to welcome a new day. A light drop of rain touched Bishop's dirty forehead.

THE MEMORY SHELF
Irene Constantine

'Take your medicine Alice, there's a good girl.' It has been sitting on the bedside table for a while, ignored by me. How many times have I heard that request, put in different ways. Now if Mary, my favourite nurse had brought it, I would have taken it immediately; but Kathleen treats me like a child, and, like a child I respond.

Terrible things these strokes, knock the stuffing out of you, my legs are almost useless. I can no longer get up, and go at will, unless you call five yards per hour, creeping along behind a zimmer, going; and, that's on good days only. Otherwise my equipment is working normally. I've been in this retirement home for two months now, after a short stay in hospital.

Things changed quickly, inevitable since I could no longer live alone. One or two items of furniture accompanied me here; my bed, and small dressing-table. The latter holding a few trinkets. Nothing of any value there. My expensive possessions have found a permanent home. But my treasures are still with me; eight assorted articles, collected over the years, now placed together on a shelf. I can see them, when lying down or sitting up; remember the important occasions and highlights in my life.

At seventy, I've really no complaints of life's ups and downs. I've been lucky, leading a useful life and I don't want to live to be old and useless. It looks as if I might get my wish.

'What's happening today, Kathleen, anything exciting?'
'For me, or you?'
'For both of us, we can each cope with a bit of excitement, can't we?'
'I'm not doing anything except work,' Kathleen replies, 'I suggest you have a quiet day, there's a trip out tomorrow. Remember, senior citizen's slide show and tea; at their meeting place.'
'Oh yes I will, I'd forgotten all about it.'

This home on the outskirts of a small town, is a happy place, housing about forty residents. We're like a large family really, enjoying trips out, drives round the countryside, visits and entertainment from local schools and groups in the area. Life is not dull by any standards, we're not encouraged to sit and mope.

I have enjoyed myself today, it was nice to see new faces, chat to them in different surroundings.

'What have you been doing today?' Mary asks in the evening. She is back on nights, where I like her to be. We've had several chats when I couldn't sleep, and when she could spare the time.
'I've been to Tipperary,' I reply.
Mary laughs, waiting for an explanation.
'Well sort of, we've been wandering round Ireland, at the slide show in town, and a nice wander it was; beautiful scenery and a nice tea to follow. Ah yes, I'd forgotten that, so you should,' I tell her, 'enjoy yourself, don't think about us when you're off duty.
'Right, madame, permission granted, I won't.'
'Doesn't that vase sparkle?' she says, changing the subject.

My room is softly lit with a lamp, placed near the memory shelf. The small crystal vase in question is filled with heather. I've brought my beloved moors into the room with me; in the warmth of this room, the heather has turned brown. But at home in a cool spot, it always keeps its colour from one summer to the next, when it is replaced.

'Did I ever tell you how I came to get that vase?'
'No, you didn't, you've told me about some of your treasures, but not that one,' Mary replies.
'That's my friendship memory, it was given to me by a dear friend, whom I haven't seen for many years. I would like to see her again, just once more, but it's not likely, I don't know where she is now.'
'What's her name?' Mary asks.
'Margaret Hartley now, she was living in Lancaster last time I saw her, but that's years since.'

Mary leaves and I have a peaceful night, sleeping well. Sister looks in next morning and Mary pops in to see what I want for breakfast.
'It's an egg this morning Alice, how would you like it cooking?'
'Fried please, kill it first, I don't want it screaming in the pan. I don't like cruelty to eggs.'

Sister looks amazed, but Mary smiles, going off to the kitchen, knowing exactly what I mean. I don't like runny yolks. She will stab it and I will be presented with a nice firm egg, leathery, just the way I like it. Sister would think it revolting, but she won't be eating it, will she?

'What are we doing today?' Sister asks, 'we're obviously in a good mood.'
'We are, I'm in a matchstick mood today. I'm going to play dominoes with Helena and friends. I'm down to three matchsticks, I want to win some back.'

With that remark she leaves and I await my egg in peace. I have a restful morning and, after lunch, the wheel-chair and I are taken downstairs in the lift. I enjoy the afternoon, winning some games, losing some, and ending up with five matchsticks. A slight improvement.

Kathleen isn't impressed with my treasures, unlike Mary, who often looks at them and chats to me about some of her memories. Contrariwise I draw Kathleen's attention to them.
'You don't think much of the memory-shelf do you?' I ask her.
'Well, it's alright I suppose, we don't all think alike do we?'
At least she's honest I think.
'True, but there's a lot of me there, the seven loves of my life are there. My love of children, animals, nature, God, memories of youth, gifts and sport.'
'I suppose that's where the cup comes in, sport,' she says, 'tell me about it Alice.'
Good, she's showing interest at last, I think. It's just a very small silver cup on a black pedestal, bearing an inscription and the date when it was won, in 1947, a long-ago sports day. It was paid for by my schoolfriends. It was my third win, but being wartime, well just after, the school could not afford another one. But that means more to me. It's filled with many memories, days when I could use my legs.

'Did you win many races?' she asks.
'Some, but it was at jumping I excelled. These old legs would joyfully leap high in the air, or hop, step and jump into a sandpit.'

'You must think positive, Alice, forget your ailments, think of the sandpit.'
'I will, I'll surprise you one day, jumping over my zimmer.'
Kathleen goes out laughing, she doesn't laugh often enough. I suppose she also has problems.

Mother's Day is approaching and I glance across to my memory shelf, looking at two of my treasures, a photo and a card, a lot of my adult years there. The card has Auntie's Day written there in a childish hand. How well I remember the day Louise, my great niece (an artistic child) gave me the card, and the story behind it.
'We're making Mother's Day cards at school, Aunty,'
I'm aunty to all of them and to other people also, it's like a third name, but I digress, back to my story. Louise went on to say that when she had finished her mother's card, she had time to spare and the teacher thought this a good idea. On the following Sunday, I was also given a party and the photo, a memory of them as they were on that day; my beloved younger brother, whom I used to protect as a child and his dynasty, children and their children, who had given me so many auntie's days.

Later, when Mary comes on duty she is thinking on the same lines.
'It will soon be Mother's Day Alice, would you like me to spruce up Isaiah Bear, give him a bath?'

'Yes please, you can't dust Isaiah, can you, and he does look a bit grubby.'
'I won't let him catch cold,' she says, 'I'll dry him well and put him in the airing cupboard for a while.'

'Thanks, you are a treasure and he won't mind the dark, bears hibernate.'
We are both on the same wavelength and very nice it is too. Isaiah is not your conventional brown bear. He's small in size, about six inches in length, with yellow legs and a white chest. He's a handsome wee fellow.
'You've never told me the history of Isaiah, I'd like to hear it,' Mary says.
'So you shall, I remember very clearly the day Isaiah came into my life; I was wandering round Woolworths with my nephew, James, and nieces

Annabelle and Eva. It was their annual Christmas shopping spree, lunch as well, my treat. James was probably about seven.

'I'm buying you a teddy, Aunty,' he said, 'then you'll have someone to sleep with, you won't be lonely.'

'Thanks' I said, somewhat taken aback, 'that will be nice.'

We looked around and he chose Isaiah, five shillings he cost, quite a lot from James' pocket money.

'He's a bit small,' I said, 'I know, I'll pin him above my bed, suspend him with a ribbon, then he'll watch over me and if we're both awake during the night, we can have a conversation.'

James agreed and Isaiah spent many years there. James also slept there when he visited his granny and I. I expect they also had conversations.

'That's a nice story Alice, I like it,' and with that remark, she goes. Two days later and Isaiah is back on the shelf, wearing a new ribbon, he's had several over the years. Very smart he looks.

I am being made a fuss of today, for some reason I cannot fathom. I have a refreshing perfumed bath. I have to be hoisted in these days. Ablutions over, Mary chooses one of my prettiest dresses, then my hair is set by the visiting hairdresser, the full treatment. Mary holds up a mirror, 'There, you look lovely,' she says.

'Thanks, I appreciate your efforts, I feel lovely.'

Once long hair, dark brown and shining with health, now short and grey, faded blue eyes. It's a good job I'm not taking this old body with me to Heaven or t'other place, departed friends from my youth wouldn't recognise me.

My chair is placed near the window, close to my memory-shelf. I can see trees and lawns, watch visitors coming up the drive. It's a blustery, grey day; March at its worst, no sun; no birds, perching on the bare sycamore branches. Only the other day, a blue tit was there and a sparrow. I glance at my vase of heather. My moor will be in a sober mood today, wearing its brown and pinky-fawn dress; the brown the smudges of heather, the pinky-fawn, the sleeping grasses dreaming of spring and summer. I've enjoyed the moor in all her moods, in all her dresses. I look at the blue walls of my room, sky-blue, a summer day. I close my eyes, imagining my moor in its almost-autumn dress.

Larksong fills my room, the hum of bees, the scent of heather. I fall asleep to dream of my moor. I am a young girl again, walking there, face lifted to the breeze, long hair blowing, my moor wearing its purple dress; vibrantly alive. Cotton grass is waving to me from its home in the damp, mossy area, close to the brown peaty-pools. Then refreshed and uplifted, I awake, stretch and open my eyes.

I have a visitor, who looks vaguely familiar. 'Surprise Alice!' that's Mary talking.
'Hullo Alice,' says the visitor.
I know that voice. It can't be; it is.
'Hello Margaret,' it's my long lost friend;
Mary leaves us to our memories. 'Do you remember?' That's Margaret talking.
'Yes I remember,' and so it went on. So many memories, then tea for two in my room, then Margaret leaving with the promise of a return visit, something for me to look forward to. It was a lovely, lovely day.

'That was a kind thing for Mary to do,' I say to Kathleen, 'finding my friend for me, did you know about it?'
'Yes I knew Mary had advertised in a magazine and paper. It was in the magazine she saw the advert.'
'I'd like to give Mary a surprise, a nice one. What do you think, have you any ideas, does she want anything?'
'That's a nice thought. She likes a surprise, and it's her birthday soon I wonder . . .'
'What do you wonder, go on, fire away. I haven't eaten anybody yet!'
'I remember you saying you've done a lot of crocheting, can you still do it?'
'Of course, I use my fingers, not my toes, why?'
'There's a pattern Mary likes in your magazine, this one.'
'That's pretty' I say as she shows me. 'Yes, I can do that, if I know her size, and if you can bring me a hook and cotton in.'
'I'll get those for you, white cotton I think she likes that, and she's the same size as me.'

So it is arranged, and I am soon crocheting busily. It is nice to be useful again, and to think my efforts will give pleasure. Fortunately for me (but not Mary) she is off work ill, so I do not have to worry about her popping in and spoiling the surprise.

There've been many cats in my life over the years, but now one only remains; a blue china one sitting tall and proud, on my memory shelf. It was bought for me by Eva, my niece, also a cat lover, paid for with money from her first wage. I was touched at the time.

Thinking of gifts reminds me of the trinkets which once lived in the now empty box on my shelf. Hand carved, it is a thing of beauty in its own right. I remember the givers as well as the trinkets, and some of the occasions when I enjoyed them. My thoughts move on to their new owners, hoping they too will enjoy them on happy occasions.

My crocheting is coming along well, no hitches there. Kathleen inspects it from time to time, holding it up against her. She also is becoming a good friend, I have misjudged her. Now when she brings my medicine I drink it immediately.

Easter approaches, cold but sunny weather. Daffodils are growing on the lawn outside my room, birds are flitting about, with bits of wool or twigs in their beaks. New life in the outside world, new hope. I look at my seventh memory thinking of their creator. A plain wooden cross looks at me; 'the last shall be first'. Here is a reminder of the man I talk to every night. A silent conversation. We have a service on Easter Sunday. Each of us receiving a small egg. I haven't been given an Easter egg for years.

'Your present will be ready for Mary's birthday,' Kathleen says, 'I can't wait to see her face.'
'Neither can I. I do hope she likes it.'
'She will.'

I finish it a week before the day, Kathleen taking it home to press, promising to bring in some wrapping paper, and a card. 'It fits perfectly' she tells me. 'I popped it on before pressing.' She hides it for me in a drawer, I will wrap it later. There are just two days to go, and I am quite relieved. I haven't been feeling so well. I hope disaster isn't going to strike just yet; a vain hope - it does, and this time it's fatal; the day before Mary's birthday.

Mary and Kathleen are performing their last duties for me. The young nurse I have loved from the beginning, and the one I have come to love. The birthday present is sitting on a chair, all ready wrapped. I'm over here by the memory shelf, that thing on the bed isn't me, I silently tell them.

Duties finished, Mary says 'What a shame, there's a parcel there unopened!'
'That's for you, for your birthday' and Kathleen passes it to Mary.
'I'll leave you with her for a moment, I know how you feel.'
Kathleen leaves, and Mary comes over to my memory shelf, hugging the parcel to her, a tear on her cheek.
'Don't cry for me,' I want to say, 'your tears should be tears of happiness.'

Then just for a moment, for the first and last time, we stand together.
Straight and tall, each taking a farewell of the memory shelf.

FLASHBACK
Rebecca Hardie

Rachel was casting her mind back. She had found some scribblings in a notebook, depicting the desperate search for clarity when the world had made no sense. *'The counsellor suggested that I am asexual. Can this be true? May be I have mistaken some feelings for others regarding men. But I thought I was normal. I think I have fancied boys . . . '* Rachel turned the page. *'It came as a shock to be told that I am like a little girl. No one ever said that before, quite the opposite in fact . . . Another shock was the counsellor's suggestion that I don't want to get better. I thought I did! No one wants to be like this.'*

And so it went on. And so Rachel found herself back in the little white attic room at the top of the stairs, with the large box of tissues on the table. Were they in case, she cried? Because if so, she did not care to oblige. Not for her counsellor. She spent much time fixing her eyes on the ceiling or the innocent Impressionist prints on the walls in their bad frames. Why should she say anything? The counsellor wasn't talking. And what did she know anyway? Regurgitated psychobabble.

Rachel noticed that the counsellor was rubbing her hands over her eyes. 'Do you have a headache?' she asked, trying to be polite.

The counsellor gave Rachel an enquiring look then leaned back in her chair, stretching a bland smile over her face. 'No,' she said, 'I was thinking. That's the way I think. Would it bother you if I did have a headache?'

'N-no,' Rachel answered, uncertain as to whether this was the right thing to say.

The counsellor appeared thoughtful. Rachel decided not to renew the dialogue, and there was a protracted pause. Until Rachel could no longer stand it. 'Will you please *say* something?' she broke in.

'What do you want me to say?' asked the counsellor, annoyingly.
'I don't know! Anything! Just don't sit there staring at me.'
'I'm not staring at you.'
'Yes you are.'

'Alright, I'll try and look some other way then. What do you want me to look at?'

Rachel could have pulled her hair out. 'The Monet.'

There was silence again, but this time the counsellor spoke first. 'Are you uncomfortable with silence?'
'Yes. Aren't you?'
'No, not always. Is it always very important to talk at home, say at the dinner table?'
'What?' Rachel could hardly believe it. 'Of course not!'
'Perhaps then you should learn to be more comfortable with silence,' said the counsellor. 'I like to think that this room is a space, in which one can just *be*. That includes being in silence.'
'I'd rather we talked,' said Rachel.
'Maybe the creativity is in the spaces between the words,' the counsellor replied, sagely.

Rachel tried not to wrinkle her nose as various obscenities entered her head. She examined her fingernails. Hm, room for improvement there. 'Does my whole problem, then revolve around my father?' she asked suddenly.
'I'm sure that he is a significant figure in your life but I think that there are issues with your mother too.'
'Like what?'
'That's something that you have to work out for yourself,' said the counsellor, infuriatingly.
Rachel decided to pursue the matter. 'Well, I've read some stuff about early feeding relationships and I don't think that any of the negative things apply to me. I mean, I wasn't deprived. In fact, I used to take too much milk.'
'So your mother *forced* milk on you!' the counsellor exploded.
'NO!' Rachel tensed right up.
The counsellor ignored this, and proceeded snappily, 'And you don't like breasts do you?'
'I never said that!'
'Yes you did! I remember quite clearly the first session when you told me that you wanted to look like a stick.'

'But I then went on to say that the one thing I didn't like about that was losing my breasts!'

'No you didn't. You said you didn't like them!'

'I DID NOT say that!' Rachel flopped her head against the back of her chair and breathed out sharply. She cast a conspicuous glance at the clock on the wall. They were not half-way through. Another half-hour of therapeutic creativity to come.

And how exactly was it supposed to be helping? How was this supposed to be luring her away from the seductive power of anorexia and bulimia? Does sharing a silent space with someone enable you to normalise your eating habits, in practice?

Opposite her, the counsellor wore a lazy smile. She wriggled her toes and surveyed the ceiling.

It was the only help available.

Bulimia beckoned. *Lose yourself in me,* she murmured. *Drown out the counsellor and her words and silences and throw them away. I will help you . . . Come to me . . .*

A year later, the utility of her eating disorder seemed so obvious. Blindingly obvious. So blindingly obvious that someone else, with the use of simple words, had had to point it out to her. Guesswork was not effective. Rachel had been guessing for as long as she had been ill, and that was seven years. And that was time enough for the sickness to become deeply rooted in her being.

And bulimia beckoned.

TOGETHER FOREVER
D Upson

She lay between the crisp white sheets, her back slightly raised on pillows. Warm and comfortable, she smiled as the thoughts flowed through her head. Memories of childhood, playing in bare feet on the stone flags that made the pavement outside her home. Her only pair of shoes were kept for going to school. Hop-scotch, top and whip, and many more games unknown by today's children were continued until she left school at the age of fourteen years. Her smile faded a little as she remembered the teasing and bullying because she was so small for her age. Then her smile returned stronger than before. Petite is the word today she thought and her brothers punished the bullies so severely that no one tried it again.

Memories of work in the textile mill flooded back. Happy times where her size was an asset when preparing the huge looms. She could reach in where others could not. She gradually grew taller but remained very slim. Her thoughts went to flirtations with boys at the dance hall in town. No real romances just kisses and cuddles with the boy of the moment mostly forgotten the moment the last goodnight was said. She gave a chuckle, not like the hussies of today, one kiss then into bed for the evening or all night.

She dreamed on, although she was wide awake. She had flings through her early twenties. One she thought serious at the time and gave herself to him but they parted with bitter words. She had a relationship with another then realising she was being used, finished the liaison. A frown creased her face at the memory. She kept her friendships to the many girlfriends for a long while after that.

Her face changed again into the most beautiful smile as memories of the first meeting with her husband came to mind. His shyness on their first date as they were introduced by mutual friends. His gentle teasing as she guided him around the dance floor with his two left feet. He never could dance properly but he tried just to please her. They talked together that first evening until four o'clock the following morning. Their friends had gone to bed and left them.

The next day they had wandered around to see the scenery of the Lancashire hills and moors. He had always thought of the county as cobbled streets and dark Satanic Mills. They had to part in the evening for he was to return to his distant home. He said he would write. She smiled even more with memories of his first letter then there were letters each day. Sunday was always miserable because there was no post. She took a deep breath. She wrote back each day. She treasured those letters. Perhaps her Granddaughter would find them to read so understanding the deep love her grandparents had shared. Another frown, she hoped the naughty bits would be glossed over.

She smiled again. Memories of the wedding day. Not grand like today's weddings, costing the earth. A white wedding with family and a few friends at the wedding breakfast in the church hall. Why breakfast? The Minister made a speech. What did he say? It does not matter but it was amusing. Finally alone with him, strong arms around her, kisses and whispered words then the consummation of their marriage. There were many more nights like that throughout the many years of their happy marriage, as he worshipped her as she him.

Their daughter was born. Memories made her smile again as she remembered her daughter progressing through the years. The first steps, her tiny shoes scuffed and worn yet lovingly polished kept and treasured. The daughter would find them amongst the other memories, the photographs, the Rose Queen crown worn at nine years old. The swimming medallions and badges. He had taught her then encouraged her to join the local swimming club, taking her however tired he was then fetching her home. Grammar school. He went to evening classes to encourage her at homework. Driving lessons for their daughter. He had drawn the line at that. She smiled again at the memories, too many to hold in her head at one time. She frowned again, he wasn't there anymore. He had told her he would wait for her because there would be another time and place for both of them.

She closed her eyes and smiled, a very serene smile for she was at peace. She hovered above what had been her body watching as the nurses went to it. The senior nurse felt for her pulse and slowly shook her head.

The younger nurse spoke, 'She looks so peaceful and happy . . . Why?'

'Her husband will be waiting for her. He died two years ago and said he would always wait. They will be together again now,' was the reply.

Marjorie floated above them, watching as they cleansed and prepared the body that had been hers, then her spirit-heart missed a beat as she heard her name called. His voice was the same, strong but kind. Then a hand reached out and grasped hers, pulling her to him for a kiss as she remembered them, strong and passionate.

He looked at her, 'Come with me, I have a place where we can be happy for evermore, that is if you can put up with me for that long.' He gave a broad smile as he always did.

She gave him a playful punch and allowed herself to be guided across the fields and hills of Wherever Land to a neat stone cottage standing on a gentle slope overlooking a sunlit valley. Amongst the trees, birds flew with their songs welcoming her.

'This is Forever Valley, do you think you would like to stay here with me?'

The sound of excited barking, then a brown and white bundle of fur rushed toward them, threading its way to and fro, between their legs.
'Carlo the Cavalier is here too, he was waiting for me and found this place for us so we can be together again. Do you like it?'

Marjorie nodded, smiling through the tears of happiness. As long as her husband was with her to make her feel safe and loved.

THE GIRL I MARRIED
Peter S A Cooper

It all started with my telephone call to Instant Insurance plc. From their advertisement in my daily paper they appeared to offer quite tempting Life and Endowment policies.

'When you have looked through the schedule of our products which I am posting off to you,' said the voice on the 'phone, 'you can let me know if there is anything further you would like to discuss. My name is Lydia - extension 18.'

I wondered why the various insurance, investment or annuity schemes available were so often called 'products', as if the company were offering differently flavoured breakfast foods. And I had only recently stopped feeling a little disconcerted at being unable to ask politely to speak to a 'Miss Jones.' Perhaps I am slightly old-fashioned.

All the same, I derived a certain amount of pleasure from discussing my affairs with someone I could address as Lydia. I looked forward to asking for Lydia if in due course I had to ring up again as suggested. I found the name delightful and convinced myself that this would also apply to its owner if I ever met her. It was to be a very long time before I actually did . . .

* * * * *

Not long afterwards, Instant Insurance plc sent somebody to call on me at my home address. He introduced himself with an air of importance as a member of their 'team of consultative advisers.' (This set me wondering whether there could ever be such a thing as *non*-consultative adviser).

More than once during the next few weeks I rang Lydia up to ask for clarification of some additional point which I pretended had slipped my mind on the day of the representative's visit. Yet I never made the journey by bus or the underground to the spot where the Instant Insurance building stood. The reason was that I decided on a more favourable scheme offered by their rivals, Acute Assurance plc.

* * * * *

Despite my altered plans a day arrived when I felt there was a further reason to speak to Lydia. This was a lunch date. It was some months later, when I was feeling more than usually at a loose end and her voice came back into my mind. It took quite a bit of courage, though. As I said before, I am possibly old-fashioned.

I suggested Le Plat du Jour, a couple of turnings away from her place of employment. The readiness with which she accepted came as a welcome surprise. It was agreed that whoever arrived first would be sitting at a table studying a Thomas Cook travel brochure.

To my embarrassment, I was the one who arrived late, having been unexpectedly delayed. I looked round for the other 'Cook's tour booklet reader,' slipping my own now unnecessary copy into my coat pocket.

I soon found the right table and wondered what caused the slightly startled glance given me by the delightful-looking holder of the brochure after I had made a little bow and said: 'You must be Lydia!' One might have expected irritation, if anything, at my unpunctuality . . . but not surprise. However, this soon passed from my mind. We enjoyed our meal and each other's company, and Instant Insurance was never mentioned by name, as there seemed to be so much else to talk about . . although she did once casually let fall that a little while back she had 'given up her job.'

The voice to which I had become accustomed on the telephone had naturally been pleasant enough. I would hardly have asked her to meet me otherwise. But it now seemed slightly warmer and softer, with an elusive little touch of melody which I put down to a more relaxed mood where Lydia was concerned or to mere imagination on my part. Or perhaps 'Extension 18' was 'not a very good line'. as they say, and had failed to do her justice.

I was glad she was not the proverbial 'Miss Jones' I mentioned just now. That again, would not have done her justice. If office life had been still as formal as in my own junior clerk days long past her employers and colleagues, like clients and enquirers, would have addressed her as Miss Elderfield.

Not that it matters any longer, for we were married about a year later, so for these last five years she has been Lydia Harcourt.

Lydia and I have been thoroughly happy together from the very start.

That however, makes it all the stranger that every now and again, until last week, there had been some curious little passing remark of which neither she or I could grasp the significance.

Without affecting our happiness, a word would slip out, purely by chance and at mercifully rare intervals, which vaguely implied some situation that could not be considered strictly normal.

Nothing really disturbing of course. Unless, that it to say, one can feel disturbed when one gradually notices, lurking in the background of one's consciousness, a faint suggestion of some unsolved and uncomprehended mystery . . .

* * * * *

One day for instance, I remarked how lucky it was for me that six years back, when I dropped the idea of signing up with Lydia's firm, she had not taken it amiss.

'What do you mean darling?' she replied. 'You *did* finalize it with us!'

I assumed that after all that time Lydia had forgotten the exact circumstances or that my own memory was at fault. I had taken out at least two policies and negotiated a term annuity and a whole-life annuity in the course of the years, so that I did not always remember, without going through my records, exactly where I was covered for different purposes.

Later, when I examined my correspondence, it showed that I had appeared to be right in my remark to my wife, inasmuch as it referred to Instant Insurance plc. There was no Instant transaction. However, my files contained the details of an Acute Insurance policy and when I mentioned this, she reacted rather unexpectedly with the words:
'Well, there you are then. That's my firm, isn't it? Although I do have a distant relative at Instant, now I come to think of it.'

I was now feeling still more confused as regards the history of my insurance policies, but then my attention was diverted to another matter. For I was in the act of starting to play a Debusssy record on our

radiogram. It happened to be 'La Mer.' inspired by the composer's visit to Beachy Head in about 1905. After the first few bars, Lydia said:
'Not quite my kind of music darling. A bit boring really.'

I had to agree, Debussy not being one of my own favourites. Yet it was for her sake that I had actually acquired the record a long time before, thinking to remember an enthusiasm for Debussy on her part when we touched on classical music during one of those telephone conversations years ago. I mentioned this and felt hurt and puzzled when she replied 'I can't ever have enthused over Debussy my love. Besides did we really talk on the telephone before we were engaged? You may be right, but if we did, it has completely gone from my mind.'

*　*　*　*　*

Then again, there was the matter of Lydia's second name. One day I noticed she had signed some document or other 'Lydia Marion Harcourt'. A vague memory of a snippet of information given me over the 'phone in those earlier days flashed through my mind.

'I thought the M stood for Melanie,' I said. 'I may be wrong but I'm sure you once mentioned on the 'phone . . . '
'Oh you and your 'phone! Even if we ever did talk on the 'phone, I couldn't have told you my second name was Melanie, because it isn't. It's Marion!'

*　*　*　*　*

Any one of these three inexplicable incidents in itself might not have been all that dramatic. Adding them together, however, I began to feel rather bewildered.

Until one evening last week, when we had visitors.

A few hours before their arrival, Lydia told me something rather interesting, not to say curious:

'You know you got it into your head for some reason that I started life as 'Lydia Melanie Elderfield'? Well, it's a funny coincidence, because that happens to be the name of a second cousin of mine . . . or rather, was her name, because she married and became Lydia Melanie Sobieski. We have never been in close or constant touch . . . but then second cousins often don't even know of each other's existence, do they? She and I are at least acquainted. She and Jan have moved to London, so I have asked them to drop in this evening for a drink and a chat.

'It was all 'in the male line', that's why the surname came down to both her and me. And our fathers were each other's first cousins, of course, but the one who became a father last did not know the other had already chosen the name 'Lydia' for *his* daughter. The two branches of our family lost contact even then. And even if he *had* known, there was no harm in our both being christened 'Lydia' anyway! I suppose we must be thankful they did not choose the same second name too: just as well she's 'Lydia Melanie' and I'm 'Lydia Marion'!'

Soon afterwards Lydia Melanie arrived, accompanied by her husband Dr Jan Sobieski, who bent very low over his second-cousin-in-law's hand. When he gently raised it to his lips on leaving, his words of thanks, like his conversation throughout the evening, only bore a very slight trace of a Polish accent.

As for his wife, *my* second-cousin-by-marriage, whom I was now meeting for the very first time, there was something in her voice to which I felt a subconscious response.

'I was taken ill in a restaurant where I had an appointment some years ago,' Lydia Melanie told us. Dr Jan Sobieski was my consultant's 'houseman'. As I have told him more than once, if his ancestor of exactly the same name helped to save Vienna from the Turks in 1683, as most of us know, the present-day Jan saved me from illness and a certain amount of depression in 1983!'

Soon after this little explanation, my wife, Lydia Marion, went to the kitchen to prepare the coffee, saying 'Do you still like 'instant'?'

I expected to hear her cousin say something like: 'Oh yes, we still make 'instant coffee' at home.' To my amazement, however, she completely misunderstood the enquiry and replied:
'No, not any longer. *I'm thinking of leaving them.*'

My wife gave a little laugh and said: 'I meant 'instant coffee', not Instant Insurance. But you've been there so many years, like me at

Acute Assurance, where Donald acquired a policy - and also a wife, as you can see! What's wrong with Instant all of a sudden?'

'Well, I just don't get on with some of the people who've recently come into the firm. By the way, did I tell you about the prospective 'insured' who rang me up and asked me out to lunch years ago? He didn't turn up at the time we had agreed on, though. I was sitting there at the restaurant table - in that place called Le Plat du Jour. I suddenly felt unwell, got up and left and then had to be rushed to hospital. This man, a 'Donald' like your husband here, never rang up to ask what had happened to me. I was rather offended and assumed, perhaps too hastily, that he had just gone off the idea of meeting me after all. But afterwards, as you know, Jan came into my life - and that was that.'

After this it seemed to be my own wife's turn again.

'*This* 'Donald' and I actually *did* meet at Le Plat du Jour,' she said. 'I even remember picking up and reading a Cook's travel brochure someone must have left behind. When Don arrived he came up to me and said 'You must be Lydia!' I assumed he had been expecting someone else called 'Lydia' who hadn't turned up. I said 'Yes I am!' Wicked, wasn't I? But I liked his voice and liked the look of this man you see here. (Can't think why!) So I thought: Oh why not? Well, after all, I *am* a Lydia, so I wasn't actually lying, was I?'

Even before my wife Lydia Marion had finished speaking her cousin suddenly went quite rigid. In dead silence she slowly turned her face, looking with intensity in my direction . . .

* * * * *

The instant coffee in your cup, Lydia Elderfield-Sobieska, had long gone quite cold. Yet you remained entirely motionless.

Puzzlement, amazement, incredulity, then realisation filled the look which bridged the space between your eyes and mine.

It was how I would picture the look of a person struck dumb and compelled by some force to stare on and on forever.